I0580795

The Real McCat

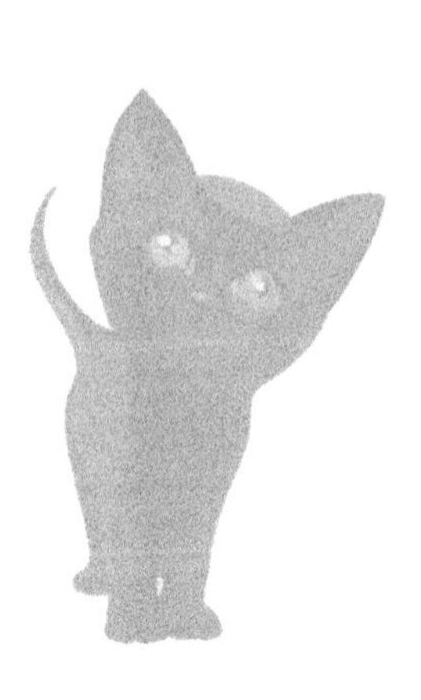

The Real McCat

PEPPER MCGRAW

P
M
G
Publishing

One

BYGUL WAS THE top matchmaker at Pawsitively Purrfect Matches. Of all the matchmaking cats in the place, *he* was legendary.

Until recently, however, this hadn't been a good thing. In fact, the other cats had looked down on him for meddling in human affairs, which as far as he was concerned, made no sense at all.

After all, their entire mission at PPM was to match homeless cats to their purrfect human companions. If this wasn't already meddling in human affairs, he didn't know what was.

Meddling or not, though, Bygul took great pride in bringing his matches to the next level. Not satisfied to simply match his cats with a human companion, he also insisted on mate-matching those humans as well. After all, PPM *was* in the business of happily furever afters.

Besides, being the cat companion of a goddess gave Bygul insight and skills the other matchmaking cats lacked. Skills that honestly made him a matchmaking genius, one who brought endless joy to the world.

So Bygul did what he did best.

He matched cats to their human companions and he matched their companions to their true mates. It was the whole true love thing that most of the other cats (and to be entirely honest, the goddesses as well) objected to.

Bygul had his suspicions as to why the goddesses objected the way they did. He had no doubt it had something to do with power and control. True love, after all, should be the purview of the gods and goddesses (and the occasional demons and demonesses), but as Bygul continually pointed out, he was the cat companion of a goddess, and therefore, he acted on her behalf whenever he mate-matched a human.

He wasn't sure Freyja completely agreed with his logic, but she didn't try to stop him either, so as far as he was concerned, that was as good as giving him permission.

Then, he made the match of the ages.

A human, so completely withdrawn from the world, that matching her to a cat was a true challenge. Yet, Bygul managed to match her in such a way that she forged bonds, not just with the cat, though she did, and not just with her true mate, though she did that as well, but also with an entire community of shifters.

Suddenly, everyone at PPM was realizing what Bygul had always known: he truly was a matchmaking genius.

Now everyone wanted his advice and half the cats at PPM had it in their heads that they too could bring true love to the masses.

And that's when Bygul's genius backfired.

Ceridwen, that interfering goddess from hell, came up with the brilliant idea that Bygul should offer mate-matching classes for the cats interested in expanding their services.

Ridiculous.

Bygul had tried to protest, explaining that it was an innate ability, not something one might learn, but Bastet had smirked and agreed with Ceridwen that this was a fabulous idea.

Freyja, outnumbered by the other two, had sighed and agreed.

So now, five times a week, Bygul was responsible for teaching an hour-long class on mate-matching humans.

He blamed the human, Maggie.

If she hadn't been so stubborn and difficult to match, no one would have recognized his genius and he could have continued to mate-match under the radar and been perfectly content. Instead, he was standing in a giant classroom at the center of Pawsitively Purrfect Matches, trying to wrangle fifty matchmaking cats into a semblance of order.

"For goddess' sake, Tivali, would you settle down?" Bygul bellowed as Cleopatra's idiotic cat companion barreled around the room, chasing some unknown demon only she could see.

This was going to be a nightmare.

"FOR GOODNESS SAKE, MAGGIE!" JEFFERSON bellowed. "Stop being so rude to the customers. You'll drive all my business away!"

Maggie glared at her brother-in-law. He had a lot of nerve, complaining about her customer service skills. "You do realize I'm only doing this as a favor because you're my mate's brother and he begged me to help you out. So really, I'm doing this as a favor to him, so he doesn't have to listen to you whine anymore."

"Yes, well, I had no idea this favor would involve you hanging up on my customers—"

"He was rude!"

"—insulting their vehicles—"

"It's ugly as sin!"

"—and refusing to answer the phone more than once an hour!"

"It rings entirely too often!"

"How is this any better than me not having a receptionist at all?"

"I don't recall promising it would be any better. In fact,

I'm pretty sure I said I couldn't promise to be personable or friendly or even to do a good job."

"I thought you were joking!"

"Well, I wasn't. And frankly, if you don't want me to be rude to your customers, then you should recruit a better set of them. I have no idea why you can't just stick to customers from our own town."

Jefferson let out a furious growl, then spun around and stormed out of the office, probably back to the bay where he was working on some useless sports car. At the last moment, he yelled over his shoulder, "And stop painting your nails in my office. It reeks!"

Maggie grinned down at her nails. They were now a beautiful shade called Lucky Lavender and they were a perfect match to the flowers on her skirt. Who cared about scents when the result was this awesome?

She supposed she should feel bad about driving Jefferson crazy and about being rude to his customers and possibly losing him some money along the way, but really, she just didn't.

Because as far as she was concerned, none of this was her fault. In fact, she'd told both Jackson and Jefferson that they wouldn't like the results of her doing this favor for them, and they just hadn't listened.

Okay, so Jackson *had* warned her that Jefferson's shop was a ways out of town, at a crossroads between three different towns, and that one of those towns was full of humans, but that didn't mean Maggie had to like it.

She thought she'd left the whole customer service, dealing with strangers, human existence behind! Yet here she was, helping out her brother-in-law doing a job she didn't need and that she absolutely hated, just because her mate had asked.

This was what getting mated got you.

Fabulous sex, incredible friendships, romantic picnics, a big brother and *favors*.

A nudge on her arm ended Maggie's stewing. "Oh, Genghis Khat, you're so sweet." She leaned over and kissed the gray forehead of the best cat in the entire world. "Sorry for all the yelling, sweetie pie. And sorry we're stuck here in this ugly monstrosity of a building, instead of back at home in our awesome garden. Give it a few more days though. I may be his sister-in-law, but I guarantee Jefferson won't last much longer. He'll fire me before you know it."

"Um, excuse me?"

A woman stood in Maggie's office door, looking uncertain. She had short, black hair that kind of spiked outward in a really sassy way and was dressed in jeans and a tee-shirt.

"I saw the help wanted sign and—"

Maggie leapt to her feet. "Come in, come in. What's your name?"

"Kate Worcester."

"Nice to meet you, Kate. I'm Maggie. So, tell me what your qualifications are."

"Oh, well. I don't really have any. I mean, not as a mechanic anyway."

"Good because what we need is a receptionist."

"Oh, well, I don't exactly have receptionist experience either, but—"

"No problem." As far as Maggie was concerned, experience didn't really count for anything. After all, *she'd* worked as a receptionist plenty of times, but was absolutely *not* qualified for the job.

In fact, despite all her work experience, Maggie had *negative* qualifications, which meant that Kate, who probably had social skills, was higher than her on the qualifications ladder. "You're hired."

Kate's eyes widened. "Oh. Wow. Well, great. I mean—are you sure?"

"Absolutely! Okay, here's the deal. The phone rings and you answer it. Make appointments if they need one. Answer questions. If you don't know the answer, make something up."

Kate raised an eyebrow.

"Okay, no, probably don't do that. Just ask Jefferson. He's the boss."

"Um. Okay."

"I think that's it. Have a great rest of the day. The hours are eight to six, six days a week. You get Sundays off. If you need anything, well—just ask Jefferson." Maggie grabbed her bag, scooped Genghis Khat into her arms and headed for the door.

Kate swung around and followed her. "So what do I say when I answer the phones?"

"I usually just say whatever comes to mind. Usually hello. Sometimes car central or mechanics-r-us or whatever." Maggie wrestled the office door open and stepped through.

"Wait. Is that the name of the shop?"

Maggie threw a grin over her shoulder at Kate. "Nope. Never bothered to learn what it is. You could ask Jefferson that as well. He probably knows. Good luck!" With that, she let the office door swing shut behind her and bounced down the two steps leading into the garage.

Dropping a kiss onto Genghis Khat's head, Maggie giggled and whispered, "Let's go tell Jefferson the good news."

JEFFERSON FELT LIKE HE WAS LOSING HIS MIND AND might come unhinged at any moment. This was all Jackson's fault. He should have known not to trust his idiotic brother.

What a terrible idea, hiring Maggie as his temporary receptionist. What had he been thinking? He'd been desperate, true, but surely not *that* desperate? And now what was he going to do? Fire her?

Jackson would never forgive him.

Then again, if Jefferson was stuck with Maggie for the rest of his life, *he'd* never forgive Jackson.

"Jefferson, you're all set," Maggie called as she swept through the shop, Genghis Khat hanging over her shoulder.

Jefferson swung away from the car he was working on to glare at Maggie. "What's that supposed to mean? I'm all set for what?"

Was she leaving in the middle of the day? He didn't know whether to celebrate or mourn if that was the case. He had no one to cover the phones, but then Maggie barely covered them anyway, so it wouldn't be much of a loss.

"Your new hire's in your office, all ready to go."

"New hire? What new hire?"

"The receptionist I just hired for you." Maggie grinned at him as she walked out the bay doors and headed for her car, calling back over her shoulder, "You're welcome!"

Jefferson shuddered. What now?

Who could she possibly have hired in the fifteen minutes since he'd last spoken with her?

He stormed across the garage and bounded up the two stairs leading into the office, muttering, "I bet she hired some bum off the streets," as he slammed through the door.

Just inside the office, he stumbled to a halt, stunned at the sight of the woman sitting at his receptionist's desk.

"I assure you I am not a bum," the woman informed him.

Speechless, Jefferson just nodded, then turned and stormed back out of the office into the shop.

She'd hired a bear! And not just any bear, a freaking grizzly! And not just any grizzly, but Kate Worcester, of the ritzy, real estate Worcester grizzlies.

High maintenance, snooty as hell, full of themselves Worcesters.

Jefferson had never actually met Kate Worcester before, or really any of the Worcesters, but that didn't mean he didn't know about them.

Rich. Spoiled. Completely detached from their own roots. He doubted a single Worcester had ever run through the woods in grizzly form, let alone shit in them.

And Kate Worcester was supposed to answer his phones?

What the freaking hell?

WELL, THAT WENT WELL. KATE ROLLED HER EYES.

If that was Jefferson, she was probably in trouble.

A search through the paperwork on the desk had turned up a number of invoices with JH Automotive at the top, so she had at least one question answered.

There were so many others, though.

Like why she was working there in the first place.

Sure she'd walked in and asked for the job, but that was beside the point. She'd just been so angry and then she'd seen the sign. It had seemed like a message from the gods.

But now that she had a minute to think about it, she was

realizing there was no way she could do this job *and* everything else. On the other hand—

At that moment, her cell phone began to ring.

Great.

She considered ignoring it, but no. He'd just do something really obnoxious, like invade her privacy and track her down.

With a sigh, she dragged out her phone and connected it, but didn't say anything.

"Well?" Mason bellowed after a few seconds.

Kate swallowed a giggle. "What? You called me."

"So you don't even bother saying hello anymore?"

"It seemed unnecessary."

"Unne—whatever. Where are you?"

"Oh, didn't you get my note?"

"You couldn't possibly be referring to this ridiculous post-it note that says 'I quit,' now could you? I know that can't be right because my sister would never walk out on the family business that way." Mason's voice rose as he spoke until he finished with a very bear-like roar.

Kate raised an eyebrow. "I don't see why not. I made it very clear, Mason, that one of these days you would go too far. Well, that day is today!"

"Oh, come on, Kate, it wasn't that bad."

"You threw the alpha of the McDonald clan out the window! Of a two-story building!"

"Eh, I'm sure he landed on his feet."

"That's not the point. And they're wolves not cats!"

"He was flirting with you."

"He was negotiating to buy the Wheeler property!"

"Oh."

"I was this close to offloading those acres, then you came along and ruined everything."

"Well, that'll teach him to keep his distance when negotiating."

"Oh, please."

"So when are you coming back?"

"What do you not understand about the words, 'I quit'?"

"You can't quit, Kate. You're not a quitter. Besides, we need you."

"Well, I'm sorry, but I've already got another job."

"You what?"

"I've given my word and have already started, and you're right. I'm not a quitter. There's no way I could leave them in the lurch, now is there? Not after they've gone to all the trouble of hiring and training me." Kate hit the mute button so he wouldn't hear her snickering.

"Training—you only left the building an hour ago!"

Kate cleared her throat to get rid of any telltale amusement and hit the mute button again. "Who said anything about the training happening today?"

Mason let out a growl. "You're making this up, aren't you? You couldn't possibly have found a job and been trained in the hour since I last saw you."

"I certainly am not making this up. I'm the new receptionist at JH Automotive."

"Receptionist? Now I know you're joking! There's no way you'd take a measly—hold on a minute. JH—are you talking about Jefferson Hewitt?"

"I believe that's my new boss's name, yes."

Dead silence, then, "You went to work for the panthers?" Mason roared.

Two

THERE WAS A reason Bygul had never been chosen to teach any of the matchmaking classes at Pawsitively Purrfect Matches. He wasn't exactly blessed with patience, nor did he have a single teaching bone in his body.

His idea of teaching was to throw the cats into the middle of a situation and see if they could manage to make a match. If they did, they passed and became matchmakers. If they didn't, they failed and went off to do something else with their tenth life.

Apparently, though, this was not considered to be good teaching.

Bygul didn't care though. After all, he'd never claimed to be a teacher and yet, he'd been roped into this nonsense anyway.

He was especially annoyed because he'd been unable to

continue his matchmaking endeavors while arguing his case with the goddesses. Then, when he'd lost, he'd spent an entire day prepping for a class that ended up involving more cat-wrangling than teaching.

He had cats to match with their human companions and humans to match with their mates, and yet, instead, he was teaching witless cats nothing at all. Not because he had nothing to teach, but because they had no discipline whatsoever and apparently lacked the ability to sit still and to learn.

The only good news was that the torture only lasted sixty minutes, and was then followed by an entire twenty-four hours of freedom.

The minute the bell sounded, Bygul exclaimed, "That's it for today, class."

"That can't be right," Muezza exclaimed from the corner where he'd been giving himself a very thorough bath. "We haven't learned anything yet!"

Bygul didn't bother to answer. He simply transported himself to his rooms, where he'd stowed his purrfect match on the way to class. "Well, little one," he said to the tiny, black kitten, curled up in the middle of his bed. "Are you ready to meet your human?"

The kitten leapt to her feet and bounced a couple times there, clearly overwhelmed with joy at the prospect.

"That's what I thought. Well, come along now. Your human's name is Jefferson and I'm sure he's going to adore you."

Jefferson stormed back into the bays and paced back and forth furiously.

It wasn't that she was a grizzly. After all, he lived in a shifter town full of bears and wolves and all sorts of different shifters. It wasn't even that she was rich.

It was that she was beautiful.

Beautiful *and* rich. Beautiful and rich and impossible to ignore.

How in the hell was he going to get any kind of work done with Bombshell Grizzly in his office?

Beautiful and rich and entirely too—

"Mew."

Jefferson froze and looked down.

A tiny black kitten stood in front of him, staring up at him.

He glanced around the shop.

"Yo, Ryan, this your kitten?"

Ryan peered around the hood he was under to stare at Jefferson. "You kidding me, boss?"

Jefferson let out a snort of laughter. "Okay. Sorry. What about you two?"

Lyle rolled out from under the car he was working on, took one look at the kitten, who was now standing on its hind legs, front paws rubbing against Jefferson's jumpsuit, and let out a snort of derision before rolling back under the car.

Pete didn't even bother to respond, just shook his head and kept working on the motorcycle chain he was repairing.

Clearly, none of them would be claiming the kitten anytime soon.

With a grunt of exasperation, Jefferson leaned over and picked it up. "What are you doing in here with all these wolves, huh?"

The kitten started to purr and rubbed its head against his jaw.

"Well, aren't you a sweetheart?" Jefferson stared speculatively at the office door. It seemed unlikely and yet, the timing—

Jefferson strode back across the service bays, leapt up the two steps, swung open the office door and demanded, "Did you bring a kitten into the shop?"

The grizzly was still sitting at the desk, staring at the cell phone in her hand. She slowly raised her head and stared at him.

The look on her face was so incredulous, Jefferson let out a huff of exasperation, swung on his heel and stormed out again. He got halfway across the bay when he realized this was probably Maggie's doing.

Fishing his cell out of his pocket, he texted her. *What's up with the kitten?*

Within seconds his phone buzzed with her reply. *What are you talking about?*

Don't act so innocent. You're the only one I know who would have the audacity to sneak a kitten into my shop.

What kind of kitten?

Rolling his eyes, Jefferson held the kitten out in one hand and snapped a photo with the other and sent it.

His phone rang.

"You'd better be on your way back here to get what you left behind," he snapped into the phone.

"That kitten is adorable. Where did you get it?"

"Oh, stop acting so innocent. You're here with Genghis Khat and almost immediately after you leave, I have a kitten. You couldn't have been more obvious."

"Are you implying that Genghis Khat had kittens while in your shop?"

"Kittens!" Jefferson roared. "Are you telling me there are more of these around here somewhere?"

"Of course not! I mean, I assume not. I don't know where that kitten came from, but it wasn't from Genghis Khat. He's a boy, for heaven's sake!"

"I know that. Besides, the kitten isn't a newborn. Just come back here and pick him up."

"No way. Genghis Khat would not approve. So is it a girl or a boy?"

Jefferson held the kitten high to take a peek. "Girl, I think."

"Yay! Give Cleocatra a kiss for me."

"Cleo—hold on a minute. Did you just name my kitten?"

"Ha! I knew it. She *is* yours."

"Hey, that's not what I—hello?" Jefferson held the phone away from his ear and stared at it. "She hung up on me!"

Chuckles from the shop brought his head up. He glared at his men. "Who wants to adopt a kitten?"

The chuckling came to an abrupt end.

"Yeah, that's what I thought. Wolves. So damn useless." He stared down at the purring kitten in his arms. "Cleocatra, huh? It's not a bad name. But don't get any ideas." He stroked the kitten on her nose. "I'm the Big Cat around here."

Cleocatra lunged for his finger, catching it between her two paws and swiping it with her tongue.

Jefferson grinned. "Okay, fine. I guess you can stay." He settled her on his shoulder and headed back toward the sports car he'd been working on. "Let's get back to work, shall we?"

Used to spending her days in high-powered negotiations for major real estate deals, Kate was rather bored.

It had taken her about twenty minutes to figure out the computer system and how to make an appointment.

It had taken her another thirty to figure out the shop's filing system (practically non-existent) and an hour to get the stacks of paperwork scattered around the office into a semblance of order.

Once this was done, there really wasn't anything to do, except answer the phone when it rang, which wasn't very often. Mostly people wanted to set up appointments or to find out when their vehicles would be ready.

She kind of winged it on both and hoped she hadn't set up an appointment for when the shop was closed or told someone their vehicle would be ready sooner than it would (she pretty much told everyone not today, call back tomorrow).

Sure, she could have gone out into the shop and asked the surly cat, but she didn't really feel like it, so she stayed in the office, surfing the net on her phone and ignoring the many, *many* repeated phone calls and texts from her over-bearing brother.

Constant glances at her phone told her that time was moving at an excruciatingly slow pace, every minute seeming to take years to tick by. This was something she was willing to endure, however, simply to teach her interfering, arrogant brother a lesson.

The desk phone rang.

With a sigh of boredom, Kate punched the speaker button. "JH Automotive. How may I help you?"

"So that's the name of the shop!" the woman on the other end exclaimed.

Kate rolled her eyes. "I found it on an invoice."

"That's great. This is Maggie, by the way. Listen, I'm not much for talking on the phone. Or really talking anytime, but I wanted to see how things are going. Not that I'll come back and help out if they're going terribly or anything, but I thought I should check anyway."

"Other than extreme boredom—"

"Yeah, I almost lost my mind sitting there for two whole days. Well, I guess it was really only one and a half since you saved me. Thanks for that, by the way."

"You bet," Kate said dryly.

"Anyway, if things are going well, I'll leave you to it. Oh, and I recommend painting your nails as one way to fight the boredom."

Kate wrinkled her nose. So that was the stench inside the office. She wanted to ask why Maggie didn't use the scent-free polishes developed by shifters, but then she realized she didn't really care. "Okay, well, thanks for checking in."

"You bet. Good luck and all that."

A dial tone filled the air before Kate could reply.

She pushed the speaker button to disconnect and sat there staring at the phone. Was this seriously her life now?

Sitting in an automotive shop, waiting for the phone to ring?

Maybe she could sneak in some work without Mason ever finding out.

Yes.

She liked this idea.

She grabbed the phone and called her assistant.

AT THE END OF THE DAY, JEFFERSON WALKED INTO the office in time to hear the grizzly say into her cell phone, "Excellent, Mr. Wong. You'll receive those contracts within the hour."

"Contracts?" Jefferson glared at Kate.

Kate just held up a hand and kept talking. "Absolutely. That sounds great. Thanks so much, Mr. Wong. You too. Bye now." She lowered the phone and looked at Jefferson. "What's up?"

Jefferson glared at her suspiciously. "What's going on?"

"Nothing at all. I've made four appointments for you this afternoon. All the details are in the system, but here's a list in case you need it." She handed him a piece of paper. "If you're looking for any papers that were scattered around the room, they're now filed appropriately in your mostly unused filing cabinets." She waved a hand toward the three cabinets he'd bought when he first opened the shop, but had given up on using within a month of opening their doors.

"Three people left messages, wanting you to call them back and I basically told everyone asking about the status of their vehicles to check back tomorrow."

Jefferson raised an eyebrow. "You can call Cecily Adams

back. Her Ford's ready for pick up. Were you negotiating a deal for The Worcester Group when I came in?"

Kate didn't reply, just stared him down.

Damn.

Grizzly sows were freaking scary.

Still sexy, but damn scary.

At that moment, Cleocatra popped her head out of the pocket on his coveralls.

Kate's mouth dropped open. "I could have sworn I smelled wolves when I arrived."

"Yeah, the other three mechanics. Why?"

"I can't believe they haven't eaten that thing yet."

"Seriously? She's just a baby." He stroked a finger down the kitten's forehead. "Don't listen to the mean ole grizzly, Cleocatra. She's just grumpy."

"*I'm* grumpy? Wow." Kate shook her head, grabbed the phone and stabbed out a number. Ignoring him, she made the call to Cecily Adams, then, *still* ignoring him, she gathered her things and headed for the door.

"You're leaving?"

She shrugged. "There's really not much going on at this point."

"You just arranged for Ms. Adams to pick up her vehicle! I need you to get her invoice together and take payment when she gets here."

Kate let out a huff. "Seriously? Is this the way it's always going to be? Nothing to do most of the day, then a ton of work right at the end when you want nothing more than to leave this den of boredom?"

Jefferson couldn't help but grin. "Only here a day and you've already figured things out. Let me know when Ms. Adams arrives." He headed out the door, calling over his shoulder, "And do something about the stench in this room, would you?"

Truthfully, the office no longer smelled only of nail polish. Now it was some weird combination of both the polish *and* grizzly musk plus some other indiscernible scent he couldn't quite make out. If he was being honest, he didn't really mind the grizzly musk and he was definitely intrigued by the third scent.

As the door slammed behind him, he heard Kate let out a roar of frustration that rattled the windows and sent the three wolves in the bays diving for the floor.

Jefferson let out a chuckle and said to Cleocatra, "Well, that's one perk of having a grizzly work here, don't you think? I can use her to terrorize the wolves."

Three

D AY ONE OF Bygul's matchmaking efforts had been a resounding success.

At first, Bygul had worried he was losing his touch as Jefferson had seemed determined to pass the kitten on to someone else.

The grizzly, the wolves, even Maggie—he'd tried them all. Luckily, none of them had agreed to take the kitten, and by the time the shop had closed that first day, it was clear Bygul had nailed it—Jefferson not only adored the kitten, he'd clearly fallen in love with her.

And so, phase one of Operation Match Jefferson was complete, with Jefferson taking the kitten home with him, thus proving Bygul's matchmaking skills were as flawless as ever.

Day two brought the bigger challenge, however: he now had to find the perfect mate for the panther.

When the grizzly had walked into the shop right after Bygul arrived with the kitten the day before, he'd actually thought she might be a good candidate, but she didn't seem too fond of cats so Bygul was reserving judgment there.

After all, she *was* a grizzly. One had to be patient when training the less evolved animals about the superiority of cats and Bygul imagined the same was true of shifters.

Unfortunately, Bygul had a very long list of cats needing matches, and even worse, the class from hell to teach, which meant he wouldn't be able to stick around the shop the way he had the day before, trying to monitor how the matchmaking was going. This was unfortunate because he needed time to figure out whether the grizzly and the panther were meant for each other.

And so, as he'd done when matching Maggie to Jefferson's brother, Jackson, Bygul recruited a helper.

Last time, it was Genghis Khat who was his partner in crime.

This time, it would be the kitten, Cleocatra.

A name that caused him endless hilarity and he couldn't *wait* to share it with all the matchmaking cats at PPM, but until then, he had to make sure Cleocatra was up for the job.

"You need to stick with Jefferson. Try to pay attention to any potential mates he encounters. I believe it will be a woman, but don't discount a man. It could really be either one. I'm currently leaning toward the grizzly, you understand, but—what? What's that supposed to mean?"

Cleocatra had a leg in the air and was washing herself thoroughly.

"Okay, so the grizzly wasn't exactly friendly. But—now don't exaggerate. She didn't threaten you. She just mentioned the terrible tendency of canines to attack our brethren. I'm sure she'd protect you from them if it became an issue."

Cleocatra stood and pounced.

"What are you doing now? There's nothing there. Nothing at all. It's air. You're pouncing on air, Cleo. This isn't helping at all."

"Okay, Cleocatra. I'm heading in to the shop," Jefferson stepped into the living room where Bygul was lecturing Cleo, scooped her up and kissed her on the nose. "Be a good kitten while I'm away, okay?" He set her on top of a cat tree and headed out.

"Oh, now, this won't do at all. He's leaving you behind, Cleo. How can you possibly mate match him if you're not with him?"

Cleo didn't seem too concerned as she continued pouncing invisible beings from one level of the cat tree to the next.

Kittens.

With a huff, Bygul leapt up onto the cat tree, caught Cleo in his mouth by the scruff of her neck and transported them both to the office at Jefferson's auto shop.

They arrived into a bustle of activity.

The grizzly, Kate, was barking orders and people were

moving furniture, setting up computers, installing what appeared to be phone lines and basically rearranging the entire office.

Bygul didn't know the panther that well, but he was pretty sure this was not going to go over well. He transported them back out of the hive of movement into the shop where everything was quiet.

Jefferson hadn't arrived yet and neither had any of the workers from the day before. Remembering they were wolves and that the grizzly had seemed to believe they might enjoy eating a kitten, Bygul wasn't certain leaving Cleocatra there without Jefferson to protect her was the best choice either.

Fine.

He'd recruit Genghis Khat as security for the kitten.

He believed this was a fabulous idea until he arrived at Maggie's house and faced G.K.'s wrath.

"I don't know why you're so upset. I said I'd help, didn't I? And I'm here, with the kitten, trying to match Jefferson to a mate, which is exactly what you wanted, right?"

G.K. gave Cleo a look of disdain.

Cleo didn't even notice. She was too busy attempting to catch the grouchy tom's tail.

Pounce. Pounce. Pounce.

The more she pounced, the more the tail swished back and forth, taunting her, yet never pausing long enough for her to catch it.

"If you really want a mate for Jefferson, you're going to

have to go to the shop with Cleo here. The job is to check out the grizzly in the office."

G.K.'s one good ear flattened against his head. The other ear was pretty flat anyway, having been mostly chewed away in a cat fight at some point.

"Look, here's the thing. The grizzly needs to learn a lesson about how superior and fierce cats are. I figured you'd be the perfect candidate for that job and while you're at it, you can check her out. See if she's good enough for our panther."

G.K. straightened a little, his tail swishing even faster.

"Awesome. Let's go then." Without waiting for a reply, Bygul quickly transported all three of them to a corner of the shop, where he left them with a quick, "Be good. I'll check back in later. I have a class to teach."

A moment later, he faced a classroom full of chaos and cats.

"There's nothing there!" He bellowed at the cats who were rolling around and pouncing on nothing. "It's not a ghost, it's not a demon, it's just air!"

DAY TWO ON THE JOB WAS MUCH BETTER THAN DAY one. This was because Kate came prepared.

Her assistant, Nick, met her at the shop early that

morning and by the time the mechanics started arriving for their shifts, the office had been completely transformed from the office of JH Automotive to the offices of JH Automotive *and* The Worcester Group.

She had the ratty old, scarred desk hauled away and replaced with two exceptional work stations, one for herself and one for Nick.

She had the phone company in, installing three new lines for The Worcester Group, she upgraded their internet to the fastest available and she had both work stations set up with sophisticated computer systems.

She even set up a Bear Necessities Station with coffee and snacks in one corner of the office that kept the mechanics visiting all day long.

It was probably a good thing that Jefferson came in late on Wednesdays, and as a result, missed all the activity, as Kate anticipated extreme grouchiness in response to all the changes.

They had just finished setting up the new computer systems when Lyle showed up in the doorway with Genghis Khat sprawled across his shoulders and Cleocatra cuddled in his hands.

"What are they doing here?" Kate exclaimed.

"Not a clue," Lyle said. "We tried calling Maggie, but she's apparently on a hike with the sheriff, so Genghis Khat is stuck with us, and Jefferson won't be in until later. You'll have to keep them in here. It's just not safe out there, what with all the equipment and tools and everything."

"What I don't understand is why an auto shop would have shop cats in the first place," Kate said.

"Yeah, this is a new development," Lyle said, "and I can't say I approve much. We sent Pete for pet supplies. He should be back soon." He dumped Genghis Khat on Kate's work station and handed her Cleocatra. "Good luck."

"Great."

"What are we supposed to do with *those*?" Nick asked incredulously.

Kate shrugged. "Your guess is as good as mine. Just don't eat them."

Nick looked horrified, which made Kate laugh.

The hours passed quickly as Kate and Nick made progress on several negotiations, one of them major, the others relatively minor, and even had time to iron out the details on a new development aimed at shifters.

Of course, the cats got into everything, Cleocatra in particular. She loved batting at all the paper and specialized in knocking over Kate's container of pens.

After the third such occurrence, Kate just left the container and pens on the floor and tried not to be charmed by the kitten, who clearly believed each of those pens were enemies to be destroyed.

With cats weaving in and out of their legs, Kate and Nick also managed to answer every call for JH Automotive, print out several invoices for customers arriving to claim their vehicles, put together a number of estimates for additional customers and, when hunger struck, order lunch for themselves and the mechanics.

As an afterthought, Kate requested a can of tuna for the cats as well.

All of this meant that on day two of her new job, Kate was most definitely *not* bored.

JEFFERSON TOOK WEDNESDAY MORNINGS OFF TO volunteer at Greensboro High School, where he helped out in their shop classes and mentored a bunch of high school shifters, who were interested in auto mechanics.

It was really one of the highlights of his week and he always came into work in a pretty good mood.

Today was no exception.

Mostly because he headed straight for the bays and got to work on one of the vehicles waiting there. All afternoon, he kept his eyes firmly away from the office and pretended he had no idea there was a sexy-scary grizzly working inside it.

He was peripherally aware that the other mechanics were wandering in and out of the office fairly regularly, but he assumed they were asking Kate to call a customer or to order a part for them.

It was only when Lyle came to ask him a question about

one of the jobs he was working on that Jefferson began to put things together.

"Where'd the coffee come from? And is that a donut?"

Lyle stuffed the last piece into his mouth and chewed quickly.

"Haven't you been listening to anything we've been saying, boss?" Pete asked. "We totally approve of your new hire."

"Definitely," Ryan called from the other side of the shop. "She makes a mean pot of coffee and did you try those brownies?"

"Oh, man," Lyle groaned. "They were delicious!"

"Yeah, she said it's Wolf Down Wednesday," Pete explained. "That means we get to wolf down snacks all day long."

"She said if anyone deserved to wolf down on Wednesdays, it was a bunch of hardworking wolves," Ryan said, wandering over with a rag in hand. "I've been trying to decide if I'm going to have another brownie or one of those giant chocolate chip cookies."

"I recommend the bear claws," Lyle said.

"No one makes bear claws like grizzlies," Ryan agreed.

Jefferson was literally speechless. He had no idea what to say. Okay, yes, he did. "Are you guys serious right now? I mean, is this a party or is it a damn auto repair shop?"

Pete chuckled. "Apparently it's both on Wednesdays, boss."

Jefferson let out a grunt of exasperation. "All I have to

say is we'd better not fall behind because you yahoos are eating instead of working!"

"Not a chance, boss," Lyle said.

"Yeah, the sugar rush has me super charged," Ryan said. "I finished the Johnson job in half the time I expected."

"Whatever." Jefferson turned back to the car he was working on. "Just get back to work."

"You should really try one of those bear claws, boss, before they all disappear," Lyle said.

The more Jefferson thought about it, the more annoyed he became.

What was up with Kate Worcester Fancy-Pants-Grizzly designating Wednesdays as some ridiculous calorie-ridden wolf-down day?

This was *his* shop, wasn't it?

He got to decide if people were going to eat inside the shop or not and he decided not.

Not!

What if crumbs got in the engines they were working on?

Or what if they got rats because they were munching down on cookies all damn day long?

After about five minutes of stewing and rapping his knuckles a number of times due to inattention, he finally gave up and headed for the office to give that grizzly a piece of his mind.

Except the minute he stepped into the office, he completely lost his train of thought.

He actually spun around to make sure he hadn't walked through a portal into a different realm, but no, that was his shop right outside the office door.

And yet, when he spun back around, the office bore zero resemblance to the office he'd locked up the night before.

"What the—who the hell are you?"

A man stood on the opposite side of the room, talking on a phone, pacing back and forth in front of a huge work station. He sent Jefferson an impatient glance, turned his back to him, and continued talking.

At that moment, Kate came out of a door at the back of the office.

For a moment, Jefferson couldn't even remember where that door led to, but then it came to him. It was a giant storeroom that he'd initially planned to use to store parts, but then he'd discovered it was more convenient for him to store the parts in the garage where they were easily accessible, and thus, the space had never been used.

"That should work. I'll have to order the part, but it should be in by then," Kate said as she walked toward a massive desk area and starting typing into the system. "Yes, that works. We'll see you then." She disconnected the phone, then swung in Jefferson's direction. "What?"

For the second time in as many days, Jefferson was utterly speechless.

"Coffee and Wolf Down Wednesday snacks are over there." Kate waved an arm toward the corner directly opposite the door he was standing in. "Otherwise, if you don't need anything, shoo. We're busy."

As if to prove her point, the phone rang and she answered it, "Kate Worcester. Oh, hello, Mrs. Simmons. Yes, yes, we received the offer. I've forwarded it to our attorney to go over it. I expect we'll have an answer or a counter-offer no later than noon tomorrow. Absolutely. All right then. I'll chat with you tomorrow. Bye now."

"What the hell—"

Kate held up a hand when the phone rang and answered it, "JH Automotive. How may I help you? I'm not sure. We're pretty backed up. Hold on a moment." She pushed a button, looked at Jefferson and said, "Can you fit in an oil change in about thirty minutes?"

Jefferson shook his head, not really in reply, just in reflex because he was pretty sure he must be hallucinating.

Apparently Kate took that as a response because she stabbed the button again and said, "I'm really sorry, we just don't have the room today. Would you be able to bring it in tomorrow? We have a couple slots available, one at ten in the morning and another at three. Three works? Wonderful. And your name? Excellent. And is this the number I can reach you at? Perfect. We'll see you tomorrow. Bye now."

The moment she ended the call, Jefferson exploded. "What the hell is going on around here? Where'd all this stuff come from? What do you think you're doing and who is he?"

"Oh, right. Here you go. My lawyer drew up this contract. I think you'll find it's quite generous."

Jefferson stared down at the paper in his hands. "Rental agreement?"

"Indeed. You do realize you don't need a full-time receptionist. You were paying an awful lot of money for someone to sit around for the majority of the day answering the occasional phone call and printing out invoices and estimates. If you'd trained your men, they could have taken shifts in the office and saved you a ton of money."

"You don't think I haven't tried that? It was always a nightmare. The men could barely handle the phone system, let alone the computers. And there's no way I want to be doing that work myself. There have to be some perks for being the boss."

"Hmm. You're telling me that those men are capable of making highly advanced automotive repairs, but can't figure out a computer software program."

Huh. That was a good point.

"I'm guessing they screwed everything up to force you to hire a receptionist you didn't need."

Jefferson scowled. They probably had. Damn wolves.

"So here's what I'm thinking. Nick and I—this is Nick, by the way—"

Nick, whose back was still turned to them, who was still muttering on the phone, waved a hand in acknowledgment and continued with his conversation.

"So Nick and I feel this is a perfect location for us. As a

benefit, it's not in Worcester Falls. We can continue to do our work for The Worcester Group without my brother's interference—"

"Would that be Mason Worcester, the Grizzly CEO who recently threw a would-be suitor out a window?" He'd heard the story the night before when the gossip had finally reached the diner where he'd eaten dinner and he'd immediately known why one of the real estate Worcesters was slumming in his shop.

Kate let out a growl that had his panther hissing in response. "He wasn't a damn suitor. We were negotiating a deal and my idiot brother completely overreacted. As usual."

"So I shouldn't be expecting Mason Worcester to storm in here at any moment and tear me and my mechanics limb from limb?"

"Well." Kate hesitated just long enough for his knees to turn to water before she laughed and said, "Don't worry. He never causes permanent damage."

"Oh, that's comforting." Jefferson glared at Kate. How had he gotten into this mess and how was he going to get out of it without being mauled by either an angry grizzly boar or an angry grizzly sow, or worse, by both of them?

"Anyway, back to the contract. Nick and I would like to rent this space. We've made a very generous offer." She tapped her finger on the document Jefferson was holding and his eyes nearly bugged out when he saw the figure listed there.

"Monthly?"

"The space is worth it. And as a bonus, you'll get Nick, and me when I'm here, as your part-time receptionists. We'll answer the phones and take care of your filing and print your invoices and estimates when needed. In return, we get to use the space and we're taking over your storage space back there as well."

"For what?" Jefferson asked.

"You'll see."

At that point, Jefferson decided he just didn't want to know. "Whatever. I'll see you later."

"Don't you want your kitten?"

"What?" He swung back around.

"I rescued her from the wolves this morning. Well, they brought her to me, but I'm pretty sure if I hadn't provided all the snacks I did, this little kitten would have been the first victim of Wolf Down Wednesday."

That's when Jefferson noticed Cleocatra was stretched out on a keyboard in the middle of Kate's work area. "How in the world did you get *here*, sweet baby?" Jefferson scooped her up into his arms and cuddled her close, eyeing Kate and Nick suspiciously.

"Oh, please. Like we'd steal your silly little kitten. Though she is rather sweet. Surprisingly so for a cat, in fact." Kate raised an eyebrow at Jefferson. "I have some pretty solid evidence that most cats, no matter how big or small, are obnoxious, cranky *and* sneaky."

"Not true, Cleocatra," Jefferson murmured in her ear. "Cats are well-bred, refined, dignified and *always* sweet."

Kate let out a snort. "How do you explain Maggie's monstrosity then?"

"Are you referring to Genghis Khat?"

Kate laughed. "Yes, and a more appropriate name for a cat I've never known."

"He's always been incredibly sweet to me. You must have riled him up somehow. How'd you meet him anyway?"

"He was here with Cleocatra this morning. Maggie came to pick him up around lunchtime."

"So that's how you got here," Jefferson said to Cleocatra. "I should have known."

"Known what?"

"Genghis Khat is notorious for escaping and showing up all over town. Not that we're in town or anything." Jefferson frowned. This was much further than Genghis Khat had ever traveled before and it seemed a bit preposterous to think he'd managed to get all this way with a kitten at his side. "Maybe Jackson's right after all."

"Jackson?"

"My brother. He blames Genghis Khat's traveling on god magic."

"I hope you're joking," Kate said. "God magic is nothing to play around with."

Jefferson shrugged. "Eh, I'm not too worried." He had much bigger things to worry about, like the grizzly who was transforming his mechanic's office into a satellite office for The Worcester Group, and her terrifying brother who may or may not want to tear him limb from limb, and Wolf Down Wednesdays.

Shaking his head, Jefferson went to leave the office, but the temptation was entirely too much.

The entire office was flooded with the scent of coffee, which was a much more enjoyable scent than yesterday's nail polish. The grizzly musk was still there, along with that elusive scent he couldn't quite identify yet, and—he glared across the office at Nick.

Not cool.

Gritting his teeth, he stormed over to the snacks table and snorted at the ridiculous sign above it.

Bear Necessities Station.

He poured himself a cup of coffee, grabbed a bear claw —because Ryan was right, no one made bear claws like grizzlies—and stormed out of the office.

As he stalked back into the garage, he seethed.

Her assistant was yet another wolf. Like he wasn't already surrounded by wolves, he had to have another one in his office?

He took a bite of the bear claw and froze.

Dear goddess of all sweet things, it was utterly divine.

He swallowed and took another bite.

Incredible.

He hated to admit it, but that sign was probably right after all because this bear claw was now an absolute necessity in his life.

Four

CLEOCATRA MIGHT BE just a kitten, but she knew when someone was trying to steal her human.

Unfortunately, she'd completely misunderstood the situation the day before.

Bygul had kept talking about finding the perfect mate for Jefferson and she'd assumed he was referring to her.

Because *of course,* she was perfect for Jefferson in every way.

But then, this morning, Genghis Khat said they needed to get serious about evaluating the grizzly and that's when she realized they weren't talking about her at all.

They were actually planning to give her Jefferson to someone else. And the first candidate was that grizzly she'd been nice to the day before.

The Betrayer.

Kate.

Well, Cleocatra wouldn't stand for it!

So, when Bygul dropped them off at the shop for the third day in a row, Cleocatra did everything in her power to make the grizzly realize Jefferson belonged to her.

When Kate was reading, Cleocatra attacked her papers.

When Kate was writing, Cleocatra chased her pen.

When Kate was typing on the computer, Cleocatra did her best to catch the words as they ran across the screen.

Cleocatra chased the phone cord when Kate was talking on the phone and chased her shoelaces whenever she was pacing the floor.

And whenever the woman turned her back, Cleocatra knocked something off her desk.

Papers.

Paperclips.

Pens.

Books.

More paper.

She even let Kate clean everything up and acted like she was no longer interested, but the minute Kate's back was turned, Cleocatra went into a whirlwind of movement, knocking everything over again.

It was really quite fun!

Genghis Khat didn't approve at all. He just sat on top of a filing cabinet and stared as Cleocatra tore around the office, causing chaos.

He did lecture her in the beginning, telling her she'd

never make friends with the grizzly that way, which was entirely the point.

As if Cleocatra wanted to make friends with the woman trying to steal her Jefferson.

It would *never* happen because Cleocatra had already claimed Jefferson as her own and that was that.

JEFFERSON WASN'T EVEN SURPRISED TO FIND Genghis Khat and Cleocatra waiting for him in the shop when he opened it the next morning.

"Seriously?" he said to Genghis Khat. "You've got to stop this, you hear me?"

Pete walked in at that moment, so Jefferson delegated. "Call Maggie, will you? Tell her Genghis Khat's at the shop again."

"Oh, man, come on! You know she's going to yell at me."

"Better you than me."

Ryan walked in at that moment and Pete was quick to delegate. "Yo, Ryan, boss needs you to call Maggie and tell her Genghis Khat's with us."

Jefferson grinned at Ryan's groan. "Come on, Cleocatra." He headed toward the bay at the end where he had a Honda waiting.

Cleocatra trotted in his wake. He found it utterly adorable, the way she followed him everywhere. The last two nights, no matter where he was in the house, there was Cleocatra, following him from room to room, sitting on his lap or on his shoulder or right next to him on the couch whenever he sat down.

"Now stay out of mischief, you hear me?"

A few moments later, Ryan reported that he'd endured a very angry Maggie yelling that they'd better take "damn good care" of her baby until she managed to come get him.

"Wonderful. Something to look forward to. Now if only Lyle would show up, we'd be in business."

At that moment, the office door opened and Lyle came trooping down the stairs, bearing coffee and—treats again?

"It's Therapy Thursday," Lyle announced.

"Therapy Thursday?" Ryan and Pete chorused.

"Yep. Kate says food is the best therapy there is, so today there's hot apple cider and coffee *plus* the most amazing muffins and breads you'll ever taste. I've already had three muffins and a slice of zucchini bread."

Jefferson wanted to scoff, but based on the bear claws from the day before, he was afraid Lyle was probably right.

The only question then, was whether he was willing to subject himself to the craziness that had become his office, just so that he could try those delicious breads and muffins.

No, the real question was whether he had the self-discipline to resist the temptation.

He tried his very best, but only actually made it about

forty minutes before he started sending his men into the office at regular intervals to grab another snack for themselves and while they were at it, to grab something for him too.

In this way, he managed to avoid the chaos of the office *and* being mauled by a grizzly because he was pretty certain, the more exposure he had to Kate, the likelier it was that he'd lose it one day and set her off in a crazed grizzly sow rage.

So he avoided the rage and still reaped the rewards of the best coffee he'd ever tasted and a truly magnificent supply of delicious breads and muffins to keep him going throughout the day.

"You know what the worst part is, Miss Cleocatra?" he said to the kitten after rescuing her for about the tenth time from a shelf full of tools. How she managed to make the leap with those tiny legs, he had no idea, but she kept doing it. "The worst part is I guarantee within a week, we'll all be sporting an extra hundred pounds."

"Speak for yourself," Ryan scoffed. "I'm going for extra runs tonight, just to work off these calories.

"I'll be working off my calories in a much more enjoyable fashion," Pete said with a leer.

"Burying the bone," Pete, Ryan and Lyle chorused at the same time.

Pete laughed. "What can I say? I'm a true ladies' wolf."

"Yes, well, do me a favor, Ladies' Wolf. Take Cleocatra into the office." Jefferson handed the kitten to Pete. "I just can't keep a close enough eye on her and she keeps getting into trouble. And while you're at it, take Genghis Khat too."

"I told you cats don't belong in the shop, man," Lyle said.

"Yes, well, if I could figure out how they're showing up here every morning, we wouldn't have this problem."

"You've clearly angered the gods," Ryan said.

DAY THREE ON THE JOB WAS CHAOTIC AND NOT quite as organized as the day before.

Somehow, Cleo and Genghis Khat showed up in the shop for the second day in a row and within an hour of opening, Pete was bringing them into the office.

"Boss says it's not safe out there for them," he said as he dropped them off.

"Then why does he keep bringing them to work with him?" Kate exclaimed in exasperation.

Her only answer was the door closing behind him.

Great.

The rest of the morning was spent trying to work while cleaning up disasters caused by Cleocatra, who seemed to have been possessed by a demon overnight.

"Weird how she's entirely focused on your desk," Nick said.

"Yeah, weird. I bet that damn panther put her up to it."

"Oh, come on, he's not that bad."

"Not that bad?" Kate stomped over to the windows that looked out over the shop. "He avoids us like the plague, but don't think I haven't noticed how he sends the others in here to get snacks and coffee for him. He enjoys all the treats we provide, but every time he looks this way, he scowls like he wants to tear us limb from limb."

"Well, you did imply your brother might do the same to him."

"Oh, please, I did nothing of the sort. In fact, I assured him that wouldn't happen."

"Yes, by telling him Mason wouldn't cause *permanent* damage. You and I both know a shifter can heal an awful lot of damage."

"But we can't regrow limbs. Therefore, I think it's perfectly obvious his limbs are safe!"

Nick let out a snort. "And I'm sure that brings him great comfort."

"So he said," Kate muttered.

"You did warn him about the contractors coming in this afternoon, right?"

"Now why would I do that?"

ONCE CLEOCATRA WAS IN THE OFFICE, THINGS GOT a little quieter in the shop, though if he were being perfectly truthful, Jefferson would have to admit he missed having Cleocatra for company.

Still, he got a lot more done without having to catsit and did his best to avoid looking toward the office, even when he became aware there was a lot of activity happening, people and things being carted in and out followed by a lot of banging and cursing.

He just kept ignoring it.

Because he absolutely didn't want to know.

He'd probably lose it if he did, thus running the risk of becoming a victim of raging sow syndrome.

So he avoided it.

Even as the other men wandered away and wandered back and began talking about scary things like shelves being torn out and walls being knocked down and electricians and plumbers and he didn't even want to know what else, he continued to ignore it all.

"Hey, boss, you should see what they're doing back here," Lyle called.

"Not interested," Jefferson yelled back.

Actually he was very interested, but wasn't about to let the grizzly know it. He'd read the rental agreement last night and had signed it despite his many reservations. At the end of the day, though, he just couldn't turn down that amount of rental money.

He'd been a bit concerned about the whole section titled

improvements, but then he'd figured whatever they did to the building couldn't possibly make it worse, and since they could only "improve" the sections they were renting, which was the office and the storage room, whatever they did probably wouldn't impact his business, so what did he care?

He was not only getting an astronomical amount of rent every month, but was also getting free receptionist work, so of course, he signed it.

He'd slid it under the office door this morning, once again avoiding the grizzly, and hadn't even thought about it since.

Until all the banging and cursing started.

Until plumbers and electricians arrived and his men started talking about walls going down and now he was drowning in curiosity and anxiety.

Damn that grizzly.

How had he gotten into this situation anyway?

Oh, right.

Maggie.

As if his thoughts had produced her from thin air, Maggie's voice thundered through the shop. "Jefferson Hewitt!"

He jerked in surprise and banged his head on the undercarriage of the car he was working on. "Ow. Dammit." One hand to his forehead, he rolled out from under the car and stared up at Maggie, who stood, hands on hips, glaring down at him.

"I can't believe you, Jefferson! How could you?"

With a sigh, Jefferson climbed to his feet, wiped his hands on a rag and asked as patiently as he possibly could, "How could I what?"

"How could you catnap Genghis Khat? You know how upsetting it is when he just disappears on me and to take him all the way out here, not once, but twice! It's not right." She glared around the shop. "Where is he anyway?"

Shit.

Shit!

Jefferson bolted past Maggie, leapt up the stairs and flung open the office door.

Kate looked up from her desk. "What?"

"Where are the cats?"

Kate pointed to the corner where a giant pet crate was sitting.

"You locked up Genghis Khat?" Maggie shrieked, then pushed around him to rush to the pet crate.

Kate shrugged. "The kitten was out of control and this environment isn't exactly conducive to cats at the moment."

That's when Jefferson noticed the door to the storage room was missing as was a portion of the wall it had been on. "What the—" He closed his eyes and deep breathed for a moment.

He wanted to be annoyed that Kate was knocking out walls, but he'd signed the damn agreement.

He wanted to be annoyed that she'd locked up Cleocatra, but it was why he'd bolted in here in the first place—

because all that banging and rumors of walls coming down had sounded terribly dangerous for a kitten.

This was why he'd avoided the offices today.

Because the grizzly made him crazy!

"You know what? I don't want to know."

"Probably a good idea," Kate agreed.

"Oh, my poor, poor Genghis Khat. Did they lock you up like a prisoner?" Maggie crooned through the cage door.

"Mrawr," Genghis Khat replied.

"Mew," Cleocatra said.

"You poor darlings. Don't worry, I'll have you out in a moment." She opened the door and Genghis Khat lunged forward into her arms.

She fell backward and hugged him tight. "I know, baby, I know."

"Mew, mew," Cleocatra said as she stuck her head out of the cage.

"Oh, you sweet thing," Maggie crooned, picking her up and cuddling her close as well.

Genghis Khat, Jefferson thought, didn't look as if he appreciated that development at all. In fact—

Jefferson leapt forward, intending to rescue Cleocatra, but Genghis Khat turned on him and lashed out with claws.

Jefferson leapt back, shocked. "It's me, Genghis Khat. I'm your friend. Jefferson, remember?" Sure, Jefferson had been terribly amused when Genghis Khat used to lash out at his brother, Jackson, but he didn't like the shoe being on the other foot.

"Don't touch him," Maggie said as she climbed to her feet, cradling both cats in her arms. "You don't *deserve* to be his friend."

"What's that supposed to mean?"

"Locking him up like that!"

"I'm not the one who locked him up! That was your new hire. Remember her? The grizzly?"

Maggie looked surprised, then swung around to face Kate. "Really? You're a grizzly shifter? I've never met a grizzly shifter before."

Jefferson groaned. "Can I have my kitten back please?"

"I don't know," Maggie snapped. "Are you going to lock her up again?"

"I didn't lock her up in the first place. Once again, that was the grizzly *you* hired."

"Whatever." Maggie looked down at Cleocatra. "What do you think, baby? Do you want to give Jefferson a second chance?"

Cleocatra responded with a tiny meow, which Maggie must have taken for agreement because she passed the kitten to Jefferson.

"Last warning, Jefferson Hewitt. No more catnapping. Got it?" Without waiting for an answer, Maggie stormed out of the office, leapt down the two stairs and stalked out of the garage.

Silence fell in her wake.

"All done in here, Ms. Worcester." A man stepped into

the room from the storage area. "You're all set up for the builders and installers."

"Excellent. And the bathrooms?"

"We'll come back for them, probably the day of installation."

"Perfect. Thank you so much, Andy."

"You bet." With a nod to Jefferson, Andy slipped by and was out the door before Jefferson could get the power of speech back.

"Bathrooms?" He croaked out. They had one at the base of the stairs between the office and the bays. It was perfectly functional and as far as he was concerned, needed no improvements.

"You really don't expect Nick or me to use that disgusting bathroom, do you?"

"It's quite revolting," Nick said. "Understandable, of course. This place *is* very blue collar. Oil and sawdust and all the accoutrements of hardworking manual laborers are certainly to be expected, but still, don't you think your men deserve a bit of luxury when they go to the restroom?"

Jefferson was once again speechless.

Luxury.

For working class wolves and cats.

In an auto mechanics shop.

Hold on a minute.

"I'm pretty sure all improvements were to be limited to the areas you rented, which did not include the bathrooms."

Kate looked surprised. "Are you telling me that as part of

our rental agreement, we aren't being given access to the restroom?"

Dammit.

"Not explicitly. It's not written that way in the contract."

"Pretty sure it's implied, dude," Nick said.

Jefferson scowled.

Damn wolf was probably right.

Blast it.

Five

BYGUL WAS LOSING it.

It was a miracle these cats had ever learned how to make a pawsitively purrfect match between a cat and a human. There was no way they'd manage to arrange a true love match between humans.

Or humans and shifters.

Or shifters and shifters.

Or whatever.

As far as Bygul was concerned, they were *all* humans.

Flawed.

Difficult to match.

Picky.

Hindered by their lack of animal instincts.

Well, the shifters had *some* instincts, but nowhere near as many as Bygul.

And so, they needed all the help they could get.

Unfortunately, if these cats were the best they could hope for, the human race was probably doomed.

Bygul had argued with the trio goddesses something fierce the day before.

It was why he never made it back to the garage to check on Genghis Khat and Cleocatra.

He'd been too busy trying to make his case that fifty cats were just too many to wrangle at once.

"The other teachers manage it just fine," Ceridwen had snapped, which really got him going, since he had never claimed, nor ever would claim, to be a teacher.

"Then let *them* teach the cats how to match a human and its mate," he'd snapped back.

"Now, Bygul," Freyja had said. "You know, they're not the experts like you are."

As if he'd fall for that bit of flattery.

Freyja should know better.

He'd spent hours arguing with them and the best he'd managed was a promise that they'd come observe his class today.

Which was just great.

He was most definitely *not* looking forward to the humiliation of having three goddesses observe his lack of control over a full clowder of cats.

What ensued that morning was chaos, as it did every morning.

An entire hour of Bygul shouting at cats to stop chasing invisible demons and to stop wrestling each other and to pay attention!

He'd get five or six listening, but then a pair of wrestling cats would barrel by and off those five or six would go.

He'd wrangle another three or four and a cat toy would roll right into the middle of their group and the next thing you'd know, they'd all be chasing that toy all over the room.

When it was finally over, Bygul didn't even have the energy to look up when the goddesses appeared beside him.

"Poor Bygul," Freyja crooned and picked him in her arms to cuddle him.

He adored being cuddled by Freyja, but didn't want to show too much joy in front of the other two goddesses, so he tried to keep his purring to a very subtle rumble.

He was afraid he didn't succeed.

"You do realize the best teaching technique involves modeling," Bastet said as she paced in front of them.

Bygul didn't even know what that meant. Was he supposed to strike a pose for the cats?

Freyja let out a soft, tinkling laugh. "Not a pose, sweet Bygul. You have to show them how it's done. Talking about it is, well, boring. Showing them, though, they might actually enjoy that."

Bygul was appalled.

Was she seriously suggesting that he bring fifty cats with him into the earth realm to assist in mate-matching Jefferson?

Surely not.

"Exactly," Ceridwen said. "I think that's the perfect solution. Tomorrow, Bygul, you'll take the cats on a field trip."

"They'll learn so much better that way, I'm sure," Bastet said.

"You'll do an absolutely fabulous job, Bygul," Freyja said, all the while stroking his back and scratching his chin and making his entire body vibrate in joy from the attention. "I just know it, darling."

"You know, the panther *is* rather cute," Nick said the minute Kate walked into the office, arms full of pastry boxes.

She gave him an incredulous look. "He's cranky and unappreciative."

She stamped over to the Bear Necessities Station and began laying out pastries. "Case in point. All these goodies we've been providing will be gone by this afternoon and the panther will certainly have eaten his own share. But will he show any appreciation at all? Of course not! And why is that, you might ask? Because he's an unappreciative jerk, that's why."

"But a cute one."

Kate let out a huff of exasperation, grabbed a chocolate

croissant and crossed to her desk, where she flopped down and glared at the computer screen.

Well, of course, the panther was cute.

She took a huge bite of the croissant and chewed angrily, thinking that cuteness should be outlawed.

She took another huge bite.

Sexiness too.

Not to mention being hot as hell.

Damn Nick for bringing it up.

She'd been doing everything possible to keep from noticing the panther's dreamy eyes whenever he stamped in here or his epic ass when he stamped out.

And now they were all she could think about.

She finished the croissant and snarled a little.

Nick grinned. "I know that snarl."

"Oh, stop it!"

He let out a hoot of laughter. "I have no idea how you've resisted temptation so far. I was tempted to flirt myself, but I'm pretty damn sure he doesn't swing my way."

Kate let out a huff. "He probably doesn't swing mine either."

"Um, I'm pretty sure that man is straight as they come."

"Yeah, but is he into bears?"

Nick snickered. "You know what they say."

Kate grinned.

"Once you go bear," they chorused together, "there's no other were."

"You should definitely give the panther a whirl," Nick said.

"Only if you make a play for Ryan."

Nick waved a hand. "Nah, that boy's way out of my league."

"You sure? Because he certainly checks you out every time he comes in here."

Nick swung around to stare at her. "Really?"

Kate grinned. "Yep."

"Huh."

Silence for a moment, then, "All right, I'll give it a shot with Ryan if you'll do the same with Jefferson."

"Seriously?"

"Absolutely."

"Okay, but don't hold your breath. I firmly expect him to bolt and run the minute I make my move."

"Doubtful. The chemistry between you two is off the charts."

"That's not chemistry. It's—"

"Yes?"

Kate sighed and propped her hand on her fist. "Lust. Good, old-fashioned lust. At least on my part. On his side, I'm pretty sure it's all irritation."

Nick snickered. "I'm pretty sure his irritation is just a cover. And here comes your chance to find out."

"Huh?"

The door to the office opened and Jefferson walked through, Cleocatra cradled in his large hands.

"Again?" Kate exclaimed.

Jefferson shrugged. "I have no explanation. Every morning, I leave her at the house and when I get here, she's waiting inside the shop."

"Maybe there are two of them," Nick said. "You know, like twins."

"I doubt it," Jefferson said, "especially considering I take her home every evening and there's no twin waiting at the house for us."

"So what you're telling us is that we're not only your part-time receptionists and renters," Kate said, "but we're also your cat sitters."

"Afraid so." Jefferson set Cleocatra on the floor and watched as she darted across the room and began wrestling with nothing he could see. He hesitated, then, "Do you mind if I—" He waved a hand toward the snack station.

"Help yourself," Kate said.

Jefferson nodded and headed for the coffee.

The minute his back was turned, Nick reached across their desks and tried to slap Kate upside the head.

She jerked back and scowled at him.

He grinned, nodded toward where Jefferson was doctoring up a cup of coffee and raised his eyebrows.

Kate shook her head.

He nodded emphatically and made a shooing gesture.

Kate rolled her eyes, let out a big sigh, then stood and headed for Jefferson. She couldn't believe she was about to try flirting with the cranky panther!

"So." She leaned against the table, set a hand on Jefferson's shoulder, leaned in and murmured into his ear, "What are you up to today?"

Jefferson froze, container of creamer in one hand, cup of coffee in the other and didn't reply.

Kate grinned. This could be fun. "I was just wondering about your tools and whether you needed any help," she paused for a heartbeat, then continued, "getting them ready for use."

Jefferson slowly set the cup of coffee and creamer back onto the table, but other than that, he stayed frozen in place, and still had nothing to say.

"What's the matter? Bear got your tongue?"

Later, Kate wasn't quite sure what happened first.

Whether Jefferson jerked away because he was totally freaked out by her flirting or if he jerked away because of Cleocatra.

All Kate knew was that she was so focused on Jefferson, she never even noticed the demon kitten stalking her.

One second, she was plastered to Jefferson's side, murmuring in his ear, the next she had a kitten on her back, front claws fully embedded in her left shoulder, back claws scrabbling at Kate's back, attempting to find purchase.

Kate let out a roar that rattled the windows and caused Nick to hit the deck and Jefferson to leap from where he stood to the opposite side of the office in one giant bound.

"Get her off me!" Kate shrieked as she tried and failed to get a good grasp on the swaying kitten.

Jefferson leapt back to her side. "Calm down. She's only a little kitten. She couldn't possibly hurt you."

His words were almost drowned out by Nick, who was rolling on the floor, laughing and crowing, "Kitten–1, Grizzy–0."

"Yo, boss," Ryan called out. "Everything okay?"

Jefferson didn't have a clue how to answer that question.

He had no idea what was going on. No idea!

"Mew," Cleocatra nuzzled his chin and gave it a swipe with her tongue.

Jefferson wanted to tell her that everything was fine and to give her plenty of praise and loving words.

The problem was his vocal cords were paralyzed.

In fact, he was pretty sure every part of him had completely shut down the moment the bear touched him. That elusive scent had coiled around him and suddenly, everything had become clear.

"Boss?" Lyle waved a hand in front of his face, Ryan and Pete on either side of him, all of them staring at him in concern.

"Jeez, Jefferson, what'd that bear do to ya?" Pete demanded.

"I think—" Jefferson broke off. She'd broken him, that's what she'd done! His voice sounded like a dying frog, not the mighty panther he normally was.

"You think what?" Ryan asked.

It couldn't be, could it?

Surely the gods wouldn't mess with him that way, would they?

"He's muttering about the gods again," Lyle reported.

"Yeah, this can't be good," Pete said.

"Maybe the bear's a goddess," Ryan suggested.

"A grizzly goddess?" Pete and Lyle chorused together.

All three of them turned and stared at the office.

"She doesn't dress like a goddess," Pete said.

"True," Lyle said. "But she doesn't dress like the rich either."

"Yeah, but if you'd asked me how a grizzly shifter would dress, I'd pretty much say jeans and a tee-shirt," Ryan said, "so maybe she dresses the way a rich grizzly goddess would."

Jefferson shook his head.

His men were idiots.

"She's not a goddess," he rumbled.

Cleocatra clearly agreed because she let out another meow and rubbed her face along his jaw.

"Well, then what's wrong with you?" Lyle demanded.

"I think the damn bear's my freaking mate."

"WELL, THAT WENT WELL," NICK SAID. "I especially loved the part where you offered to handle his tools."

Kate snickered. "He really is quite adorable. He didn't know what to do. Or say. He was putty in my hands. Then that demon kitten ruined everything."

Nick snickered. "I had no idea bears could reach that high a decibel."

"What are you talking about?"

"You shrieked."

"I most certainly did not! Bears do not shriek."

"Not usually, no, but you hit the high pitch on that one." Nick laughed. "It's a miracle the windows didn't shatter."

"Whatever."

A loud burst of laughter came from outside in the garage and Kate stalked to the window to see what was going on.

"What on earth do you think they're doing?" Nick asked as he came to her side.

"Not a clue."

The wolves were rolling around on the garage floor, hooting with laughter, while Jefferson stood over them, glaring.

Cleocatra was perched on his shoulder and seemed to

sense they were watching because she turned her head and looked right at them.

"Is she hissing at us?" Kate demanded. "I think she's hissing at us. How rude. She needs to be taught a lesson."

"No, no," Nick said. "No lessons today, especially if they involve roaring at a tiny, defenseless kitten."

"Defenseless? Did you see her attack me?"

"Yep. My guess? She knew you were putting the moves on her human and wanted to tell you 'Hands off, Sister.'"

"Oh, for heaven's sake. That's ridiculous."

"Do you have a better explanation?"

Kate let out a huff and stamped back to her desk. "You want to know the weirdest thing about the whole situation?"

"What's that?"

"My bear actually perked up when I got close to the panther."

"That doesn't sound weird at all. Sounds like business as usual. Your bear does like to size up its prey before jumping right into the maiming and mauling."

"Yeah," Kate drawled slowly. "Except that's not the reason she was checking him out."

"Wait a minute. Your bear *didn't* want to maim and maul him?"

"Nope."

"You're telling me you got close to the panther and your bear was what? *Interested* in him?"

Kate shrugged. "Or something. I honestly don't know. But it wasn't her normal reaction to most males."

"Well, this is unexpected." Nick grinned. "You know what I think?"

"What?"

"I think the panther could be your mate."

JEFFERSON HAD JUST MANAGED TO GET THE wolves calmed down when a loud explosion of laughter came from above.

They all turned and stared at the office.

From their angle, all they could see was Nick standing hands on hips, chin lowered, gaze aimed at the office floor.

He must have sensed their stares because he turned and looked out at them.

He flashed a grin and shrugged.

Jefferson sighed. "I'm freaking doomed."

Six

BYGUL DIDN'T THINK it bode well that the wolf mechanics were rolling around on the floor, laughing like loons, in response to the idea that the panther and bear might be mates.

Call him crazy, but that seemed a bit discouraging.

Especially since he was there to try and get a handle on the mating situation before all fifty matchmaking cats descended on the garage tomorrow.

That was a disaster just waiting to happen, so he was there to try and lay the groundwork so that things went as smoothly as they possibly could the next day.

But now, with the wolves laughing it up and the panther looking like he'd been hit over the head by an anvil and—was the bear laughing too?

Bygul popped into the office in time to hear the bear say

in between giggles, "My mate? Don't be ridiculous. I think I'd know if the panther was my mate."

Nick was standing beside her, hands on hips, staring down at her. "And how would you know if you haven't shifted around him yet?"

Kate's giggles tapered off, then she said, "I think my bear would have given me a clue if that were the case!"

"Correct me if I'm wrong, but didn't you just say your bear perked up when you got close to the panther. Don't you think that might have constituted a clue?"

Kate scowled. "You suck."

Yeah, this was a disaster already.

Bygul popped back into the garage. "G.K., Cleo, I thought you were supposed to be helping this mating along! What's the big idea? The panther looks sick at the thought of being mated to the bear and the bear's in total denial. How is this helping their romance along?"

Cleo, who happened to be hanging out on Jefferson's shoulder at that moment, turned her head and hissed at Bygul, startling Jefferson, who stroked her fur and murmured, "it's okay, sweetie."

She let out a plaintive meow and Bygul growled in frustration.

"What do you mean you don't like the bear?"

Cleo meowed a couple additional times and G.K. let out a sound that Bygul could only describe as the cat version of a snicker, then plopped on his side, lifted a leg and began cleaning himself quite vigorously.

Great.

Perhaps the bear wasn't the right mate for the panther after all.

Cleo seemed extremely put out, but then again, Bygul had a feeling she'd hate anyone he suggested given her extremely possessive stance on Jefferson's shoulder at the moment.

Her back legs were planted on his left shoulder, while her front legs were draped across the top of his head and every once in a while she leaned over to swipe his forehead with her tongue.

Jefferson didn't seem to mind.

In fact, every time she licked him, he let out a chuckle and tickled her on the forehead or chin or wherever he could reach at that moment.

Clearly, those two were a match made in heaven, or in this case, a match made by Bygul.

As for the match between bear and panther, however, apparently there was much work to be done there.

Either that or Bygul was in desperate need of new candidates.

"I thought you wanted a mate for Jefferson," he admonished G.K. "So what are you doing lying about, not helping this romance along?"

G.K. stretched, let out a yawn, then sauntered toward the office. When he reached the stairs, he looked back at Bygul as if to say, "Well, get me in there already."

Bygul sighed. These earth-bound cats were just so needy.

KATE WAS BACK AT HER DESK, SUPPOSEDLY reviewing an offer for a piece of property they were looking to buy a couple towns over.

Unfortunately, she couldn't stop thinking about Nick's preposterous suggestion that the panther was her mate.

Preposterous for no other reason than that she'd always assumed she'd know right away.

Not to mention she'd also assumed her mate would be a bear.

Not that there was anything wrong with other shifters, per se, it's just that life would be so much easier with a bear.

Another bear would understand her need for fuel all day long and wouldn't be surprised to discover that she pretty much only stopped eating when asleep.

And if she'd been lucky enough to mate with another grizzly, well, a grizzly would understand her obsession with nuts, fruit, fish, and well, really, anything tasty at all. It would be a match made in foodie heaven.

Unfortunately, a quick search of the internet told her that panthers in the wild might only eat once a week.

Once a week!

How on earth would they survive such insanity?

She consoled herself with the knowledge that she'd seen Jefferson partaking of the snacks she'd provided on Wolf

Down Wednesday and on Therapy Thursday, but now that she thought about it—she glanced toward the table—he'd left without his coffee and hadn't had a thing to eat during Feast on Friday.

In fact, none of the wolves had come inside for Feast on Friday either.

Perhaps they had no idea Fridays were for feasting.

That seemed terribly tragic.

She'd have to educate them immediately.

Kate stood and headed around the desk, almost tripping on Genghis Khat who was lying in the middle of the floor. "What are you doing in here? How did you get in here anyway? Did that panther just drop you off in here without a single word about it?" She leaned down and hefted him into her arms.

She crossed to the door, flung it open and shouted into the garage, "It's Feast on Friday, lads." Genghis Khat, who had been relaxed in her arms, stiffened like a board. "Oh don't worry. No cats are on the menu today!"

"Not even the panther here?" Ryan called out.

"As I said, not today, though no promises about tomorrow!" Kate whirled and headed back into the office, allowing the door to slam behind her.

"Way to impress your mate," Nick said.

Kate rolled her eyes. "Stop with the mate nonsense. Besides, if it's true, he's just going to thave to get used to my bearish ways."

"Right."

"You heard her, Jefferson, no cats on the menu today," Ryan said.

"Yeah," Lyle said. "I think that was an invitation to go flirt with your mate."

"And while you're in there, grab us some snacks," Pete said.

Jefferson groaned. "I can't flirt with her. She's a predator."

The wolves all gave him a look, then cracked up laughing.

"Dude!" Pete exclaimed.

"What are you then?" Ryan asked.

"A fluffy bunny rabbit maybe," Lyle said.

"I had no idea panthers were such wusses," Ryan said.

"Not that kind of predator!" Jefferson exclaimed. "You should have seen her. She went from cold and haughty to stroking a hand across my back and whispering in my ear about helping me get my tools ready. She was freaking out my panther!"

"Seriously?" Ryan exclaimed.

"Dude, this is going to be the easiest mating on the books," Lyle said. "Just go in there and let her do her thing. You'll be mated before you know it!"

"Right," Pete said, "and no running away."

"Maybe try and flirt back this time," Ryan said.

"Fine," Jefferson said. "But don't—" He didn't finish his sentence on account of Cleocatra who instead of licking his forehead this time, leaned into his field of vision and bit him on the nose. "Yeow!" He scooped her away from his face and held one hand up to his nose, probing it.

No blood, thank goodness.

He glared at the wolves, who were back on the ground, rolling around and laughing hysterically.

"Kitten–1," Ryan chortled.

"Panther–0," Lyle and Pete chorused.

GENGHIS KHAT WAS SPRAWLED ACROSS KATE'S desk, right next to her keyboard, occasionally stretching out one lazy paw and slapping it down right on the keys, causing a barrage of letters to stream across the document she was reading.

Each time, she gave him a scratch on the head, scooted his paw off the keyboard, erased his additions and kept reading.

They'd been playing this strange game for about ten minutes when the office door opened and Jefferson walked in, Cleocatra perched on his shoulder.

He looked nervous, Kate thought, and yet he'd returned to the office.

The question was whether he'd come back for the flirting or for the coffee.

Jefferson hesitated in the doorway for a split second, then made a beeline for the Bear Necessities Station.

Kate rolled her eyes.

Of course, it was the coffee.

She was debating approaching him to continue the flirting when Cleocatra turned completely around on his shoulder to stare at Kate while Jefferson poured a cup of coffee.

Cleo bared her fangs at Kate, who leaned forward and was about to release her own fangs when Nick slapped her upside the head.

She glared at him and he shook his head emphatically. "Make friends," he hissed.

Kate scowled, climbed to her feet, walked around her desk and headed over to join Jefferson at the Bear Necessities Station.

"So, Jefferson." She leaned up against the table and nudged shoulders with him—the opposite shoulder from where Cleocatra was perched, of course. "Where were we?"

Cleocatra leaned down from Jefferson's shoulder, setting her front paws on his chest, turned her head and hissed at Kate.

Kate let out a soft rumble of annoyance.

Stupid kitten.

Kate would never admit it out loud, but she was rather upset that Cleocatra, who had been perfectly adorable and sweet the first day they'd met, had since decided she didn't like Kate.

Kate had no idea what she'd done, but she was starting to think Nick might be right.

The kitten was emphatically staking her claim on Jefferson.

"It's okay, Cleocatra, baby. The crazy bear isn't going to hurt you." Jefferson scratched her under the chin, kissed her on the top of her head, then lifted her down to the floor.

The kitten immediately darted to Kate's side and attacked her ankle.

Since Kate was wearing jeans and ankle-high boots under them, she barely felt the kitten's claws as she scrabbled around in a circle, growling and attempting to make it through all the material to Kate's skin.

Jefferson stared down at Cleocatra, a strange look on his face.

Was that—

He glanced up at Kate, eyes twinkling and she knew it was.

He was amused!

Kate scowled.

He probably even thought the kitten's antics were adorable.

Kate peeked down at the kitten just in time to see her back legs disappear as she scrabbled around Kate's ankles. A second later, her head popped out from the opposite ankle as she began the journey again.

On her side the entire time, claws scrabbling at Kate's jeans, Cleocatra hurtled around the front of Kate's legs and disappeared once more.

Okay.

Maybe she was a little adorable.

Jefferson let out a snort of laughter as Cleocatra rounded Kate's ankles again.

Genghis Khat came out of nowhere and slapped one paw down on Cleocatra's whipping tail as she hurtled by.

Cleocatra let out a screech and leapt up. Her small body collided with the back of Kate's left knee, buckling it.

Kate slammed into Jefferson, who caught her in his arms, stumbled back a couple steps, but managed to keep them both upright.

Kate's face planted right against his neck and she got a whiff of his delicious scent, a mix of oil and man that had her blood humming.

She couldn't resist a taste.

One tiny lick.

Jefferson inhaled sharply and she scraped her teeth along the pulse point that was *right there*.

Jefferson set a hand at the base of her neck, took a firm grip of her hair and pulled her back.

Kate had a split second of searing disappointment, then his mouth landed on hers.

Holy hell.

Who knew that panthers could kiss like that?

Shivers climbed up Kate's spine as she gripped Jefferson's shoulders and kissed him back.

Their tongues tangled and waves of heat washed over Kate as she shoved him, all the while kissing him, until his back hit the wall of windows and she had him right where she wanted him.

His mouth was devouring hers or maybe hers was devouring his.

Her head was spinning with lust and she just couldn't get close enough.

One of his hands clamped on her ass and lifted her closer.

She hitched her legs around his waist and pulled herself up so she was a little above him, forcing his head back and giving her a new angle.

She ran her fingers through his silky, black hair and pulled back a little to see his eyes.

Glazed, like she was sure hers were, and full of lust.

He pulled her back and kissed her again and she lost all train of thought, all rhythm, all coordination and everything narrowed down to Jefferson and this one incredible kiss.

"DON'T SEE THAT EVERY DAY," RYAN SAID.

"What's that?" Lyle asked from under the hood of an old Chevy.

"That." Ryan waved a hand toward the office.

Lyle peeked out from under the hood and let out a snort of laughter. "Yo, Pete!" He called across the bays. "Check it out!"

Pete looked up from where he was working on a motorcycle, glanced over at what had caught the other two's attention and let out a bark of laughter.

Jefferson's back was against the office windows, the bear plastered to him. Her hands were all over his hair, which was standing on end and the two were clearly kissing.

"I'm guessing he either flirted back or found out he didn't really need to," Lyle said with a laugh.

"The way she's all over him, I'd say he didn't need to," Ryan said.

"Uh-oh," Pete said. "Here comes Maggie."

"Where is he? Where's that catnapping bastard, Jefferson?" Maggie demanded.

"Uh, he's kind of busy at the moment, Maggie," Ryan said.

"He'd better be busy taking care of my cat," Maggie retorted.

"I think he's more interested in taking care of the bear," Lyle said, pointing to the office windows. "You should come over here to get the full effect."

Scowling, Maggie stalked across the first bay to where

Lyle was standing, then followed his gaze to the office windows.

Maggie gasped. "Is that my new hire?"

"Yep," Ryan said.

"We heartily approve of her, by the way," Lyle said.

"She's kissing the boss!" Maggie exclaimed. "How is that worthy of approval?"

"Because today's Feast on Friday," Pete said.

"Feast on—what?"

"I think it's a bear thing," Pete said. "Every day of the week so far has had a theme."

"Seriously?"

"Yep. Yesterday was Therapy Thursday," Ryan said.

"I particularly enjoyed Wolf Down Wednesday," Lyle said. "The bear claws were to die for."

"You got bear claws?"

"Yep, you were here. You should have grabbed one," Lyle said.

"No one told me there were bear claws! What have you got up there today?"

"We don't know yet," Pete said. "We sent Jefferson to scope things out and bring us back some snacks."

"Well, I don't know about finding snacks for you guys, but he's clearly managed to find one for himself," Maggie said dryly.

PERIPHERALLY, JEFFERSON WAS AWARE THAT Cleocatra wasn't happy with him.

She was racing around them in half-circles, jumping at his legs, trying to get his attention, and meowing incessantly.

That was all background noise though because all of Jefferson's attention was on Kate.

Glorious Kate, of the absolutely sinful mouth, who had sent all thoughts fleeing his head with a single lick of her tongue.

He'd felt that tiny swipe of her tongue, then the scrape of her teeth and he'd completely lost his mind.

But what a glorious way to go.

The woman was simply luscious and Jefferson couldn't get enough of her.

The taste of her, the scent of her arousal, the feel of her under his hands, the sexy aggression she showed as she shoved him against the windows, all of it combined to shred his thoughts and bring his blood to boiling.

A yowl sounded from a distance followed by a crash and Kate jerked away from him with a roar.

It took Jefferson a moment to catch his breath and from there a couple more moments to realize what had happened.

The Bear Necessities Station was still upright, but several

platters of goodies had fallen to the floor and Cleocatra was firmly attached to Kate's head.

"What is up with your kitten?" Kate growled as she tried to remove Cleocatra's claws from her scalp.

Into this chaos, Maggie arrived. "Catnapper!" She shouted at Jefferson as she stormed over to the Bear Necessities Station where Genghis Khat was sniffing at all the treats that had landed on the floor.

Maggie swept him into her arms. "Don't worry, baby, we're going to the diner where we'll get you some treats that haven't been dumped on the floor."

Genghis Khat sprawled across her arms like a king in his throne and looked as content as Jefferson had ever seen him.

"Why are you wearing that kitten as a hat?" Maggie demanded, staring at Kate, who had apparently given up trying to extract the kitten's claws and was now petting her.

Jefferson wasn't sure Kate was aware that she was petting Cleocatra nor was he certain the kitten knew that her growls were starting to sound more like purrs. Still, he figured he should probably refrain from pointing out the waning of hostilities.

"I'm not wearing the kitten as a hat," Kate informed Maggie. "The kitten's wearing me as a person."

"But why?"

Kate shrugged. "Who knows? She's a kitten. She's probably got all kinds of kitteny thoughts we'll never understand."

Nick cleared his throat and Jefferson froze.

Dear shifter gods, he'd forgotten about the wolf.

Had he been there the entire time?

One glance at the grin on the wolf's face and Jefferson was sure the answer was yes. At least the wolf was standing in the doorway to the storage area, so maybe he'd been in there part of the time at least.

"I told you," Nick said. "The kitten's been warning you for days, 'Hands off my man.' You failed to listen and now you're paying the price."

"Must you always be right, Nick?" Kate demanded.

"What can I say? It's my specialty."

Seven

⌘

THE NEXT DAY was everything Bygul feared it would be.

It began early in the morning when he stepped into the PPM classroom, ready to take fifty cats with him to the earth realm.

As usual, they weren't cooperative at all.

"Settle down," he shouted at the cats milling around.

They were entirely too excited about the expedition, bouncing around all over the place.

"Yesterday, the bear and the panther kissed for the first time, thanks to my unparalleled matchmaking skills," Bygul lectured them. "Today's goal is to further that romance along, to see if the bear and the panther will suit long-term. We are *not* going to earth to play or to make friends."

"Not even one?" A tabby from the back asked.

"Not even one! We're matchmakers, not kittens. Get it together."

"Well, this sucks," a calico snapped.

"Yeah," a tuxedo groaned. "I was really looking forward to interacting with the humans."

"Personally, I can't wait to meet Cleocatra," Tivali said with a giggle. "Cleopatra was not amused when I told her what you named the kitten, Bygul."

"I didn't name her," Bygul snarled. "Maggie did."

"It's still hilarious and I still can't wait to meet her," Tivali said.

"Fine, whatever, let's just get this over with," Bygul said. "First stop is to pick up Cleocatra."

"Yay!" Tivali exclaimed.

Bygul couldn't think of any activity less deserving of a yay than carting fifty cats around while trying to make a match, but whatever. "From there, we'll grab Genghis Khat and then head for the shop. Everyone follow me."

The only good news was that Bygul didn't have to transport any of them. They could all transport themselves so all they had to do was keep up with him.

Of course, they probably couldn't, so that was the second piece of good news. If he was lucky, he'd lose about forty of them along the way.

Not that they'd be lost permanently or anything. After all, they could all find their way home again, but if he was lucky, they wouldn't be able to track him down.

When they arrived at Jefferson's place, Bygul was disappointed to see that most of the cats had managed that first leg of the journey just fine.

With a harrumph, he went to grab Cleo, to transport them to Maggie's house, only Cleo bounced away at the last moment and he missed her entirely.

Whirling around, he scowled as she tore around the room, weaving in and out and around other cats crowding the living room.

She bounced over a lazy tom who had collapsed in the middle of the floor, slid under the belly of a black cat, then bounced up and pounced on a Persian's tail.

"Mrawr!" The Persian cried out, but Cleo was already gone, bouncing over more cats, wrestling with one, chasing another's tail, pouncing on a third's back.

"Cleocatra!" Bygul cried out. "Stop playing around. Jefferson's already at the shop."

The minute he said Jefferson's name, the kitten slid to a stop, whirled and raced toward him, sliding to a stop right in front of him. She tilted her head back and stared up at him.

"Yes," he told her, "it's time to go to Jefferson now. But I'm warning you, Cleo, if you keep causing trouble instead of trying to help this matematching along, I'm leaving you behind tomorrow."

Cleo let out a pitiful meow and Bygul sighed. "Just keep it together today, okay? Everyone else, try and keep up."

He transported the two of them straight to Maggie's house, where Genghis Khat was impatiently waiting, pacing back and forth, tail swishing in agitation.

Bygul sighed. "Yes, you're right, Cleo. That's not Jefferson, but we're headed there next. And it's not my fault we're late, G.K."

At that moment, cats began popping into the room, one after the other.

G.K. let out a yowl of fury and started attacking at will.

Bygul groaned.

He should have known this would happen.

It really was too bad earthbound cats could see their heavenly counterparts. It would be so much simpler if they were blind like the humans.

Then again, if they were blind, Bygul couldn't have recruited their help for his matchmaking efforts, so he supposed it was just as well.

All over the room, cats were popping in and out, running into each other as they tried to escape a rampaging, snarling Genghis Khat.

"That's enough!" Bygul bellowed. "Genghis Khat, you did really well yesterday. Your efforts were critical in getting Jefferson to kiss the bear. If you want to help again today, you need to settle down and get over here now."

G.K. skidded to a halt, so that he was standing face-to-face with a Maine Coon who had refused to run when G.K. challenged him and who now stood, fur on end, growling incessantly.

G.K. growled back and for a moment, the room was filled with a crescendo of growls.

"Mew," Cleocatra said plaintively.

"I said knock it off, G.K. You're scaring Cleo," Bygul said.

"Oh, it's all right, sweetheart." Tivali sidled up to Cleo and began to groom her. "Don't worry. Those toms are just letting off steam."

With one last huff of annoyance, G.K. whirled around, his tail moving so fast, the Maine Coon wasn't quite able to avoid being smacked in the face with it.

G.K. sauntered up to Bygul, a smug look on his face.

Bygul sighed.

Some days it just wasn't worth getting out from under the covers.

SATURDAYS WERE BUSY DAYS AT THE SHOP, WITH so many people coming in for last-minute oil changes and other car repairs they didn't have time to take care of during the week.

They were usually fully booked with appointments, but then had a ton of walk-ins begging to be squeezed in.

It was a crazy, fast-paced day with very little time for enjoying the Bear Necessities Kate and Nick provided for what they called Snarf It Saturday.

This meant that Kate ended up making coffees for each of the mechanics and delivering them along with a plate of goodies right at the start of their day. She and Nick then continued to keep them supplied all day long.

Adding to the chaos of their typical Saturday was Cleocatra, who had apparently gone insane in the thirty minutes she was away from Jefferson.

As usual, Jefferson had left her at home, but when he'd arrived at the shop, there she was, Genghis Khat at her side.

He had no idea what was going on with her that morning, but she was full of way more energy than usual and that was saying something, consider her usual was pretty energetic.

All morning long, she was constantly racing around the shop, pouncing on nothing and wrestling with no one.

"It's like she thinks there's someone there," Ryan observed.

"More like a lot of someones." Pete laughed.

Jefferson just shook his head as he rolled beneath a Ford Tempo. He was just getting started when Cleocatra shot beneath the car and snuggled up next to him.

"Well, hello there, darling. What's up?"

She couldn't have been with him more than five minutes before she shot out from under the car and started rolling across the garage again.

BYGUL COULDN'T BELIEVE THE CHAOS OF THE garage once they arrived.

Of course, he did bring fifty-two cats with him. Yes, somehow all fifty blasted cats managed to make the journey.

Not a single one got lost!

He was purely disgusted at the sheer bad luck of that.

In any case, Genghis Khat clearly didn't consider the garage his territory the way he did Maggie's place because he seemed uninterested in the other cats.

He simply plopped down in the middle of one of the bays and began to groom himself.

Meanwhile, the other fifty cats raced around the room, chasing each other, wrestling with each other and into that chaos came Cleocatra, who had clearly made it her mission to catch at least one of the cats.

Not that the cats were going to let that happen.

They went insubstantial anytime she got near so that poor Cleocatra skidded through, fell through and ran through a number of cats without ever physically connecting to a single one.

She got close and they popped away.

Over and over and over again.

"Stop torturing Cleocatra!" Bygul bellowed. "And stop playing around. We're on a mission here, matchmakers!"

At that moment Nick came out of the office, sauntered down the two steps there and made his way across the bays toward Ryan.

"Is that the bear?" Tivali wanted to know.

"And is that the panther?" Muezza asked.

"No, no. Those are both wolves," Bygul said.

Tivali made a sound Bygul associated with furballs.

"Dogs?" A siamese named Soraya slid to a stop by Bygul and stared at the two wolves. "You're mate-matching dogs now?"

"Of course not! They're not the targets at all." Bygul scanned the garage. "Jefferson's under that car over there. You can just see his legs."

"Why is he under there?" Tivali asked.

Bygul sighed. "It's his job or something. Anyway, he's a panther. The bear's up in the office."

"I'm more interested in the wolves," Tivali said.

"Why?" Soraya asked.

"I think it would be funny. After all, they'd probably never make a go of it without a cat's influence."

"Good point," Soraya said. "I think I'll join you."

"What do you mean you'll join her?" Bygul exclaimed. "They're not the targets!"

"They're rather cute together," a ginger cat said. "Look at how they're leaning toward each other. Just a little push and they'd probably end up living happily ever after."

"Not if they're not mates," Bygul said. "Besides, *they're not the targets*!"

The ginger cat had already walked away though and with her went about fourteen other cats, all of them following Tivali and Soraya.

Bygul let out a huff. "Is no one going to observe the

match we came here to make? You know the one—the panther and the bear."

"I think we can do both," a black cat said as he sauntered by, two other cats on either side of him.

"Yes," agreed Muezza. "Let's do both."

KATE GRINNED AS SHE WATCHED NICK SAUNTER UP to Ryan and begin flirting.

Nick was an exceptional flirt.

He had body language and innuendo down to a science.

If Ryan leaned even partly that way and if he found Nick to be even minimally attractive, well, he didn't stand a chance.

Cleo rolled across the garage floor right then. It really looked like she was wrestling something, but nothing was there.

"Crazy kitten." Kate would have continued watching, but a customer arrived to pick up their vehicle and another arrived asking if they could squeeze in an oil change.

The day went by fairly quickly, with Nick and Kate taking turns wandering into the garage with refills from the Bear Necessities Station and to flirt with their chosen target.

The more time Kate spent around Jefferson, the more intrigued she became.

She adored how gentle and loving he was with the kitten and couldn't help but imagine those large hands stroking her from top to bottom the way he did Cleocatra, except with a lot more vigor and passion.

She loved his sense of humor and the sound of his laughter when joking with the other mechanics.

Her heart about melted when he spent fifteen minutes flirting with Mrs. Williams, an elderly retired widow, making her face light up in joy. He'd been working on her car off and on all week and Kate had prepared the invoice, which she'd thought was a terrible use of funds for such an old vehicle that had long since gone past its prime.

When it came time to check Mrs. Williams out, though, Jefferson shook his head at Kate, walked Mrs. Williams to her car, helped her into it, spent five minutes chatting with her, then sent her off with a wave.

He came back into the office, grabbed a cookie from the Bear Necessities Station and told Kate as he passed Nick, who was on his way back in from another round of flirting and coffee delivery, "Zero out that invoice. I've got it covered."

The minute the door shut behind him, Nick exclaimed, wide eyed, "How big was that invoice?"

"She needed a new transmission, new brakes, new belts, I don't even know what all. He was mining parts from all over the country. I have a feeling there were more costs than I know about, but what I added up came to a little over eight thousand dollars."

"Damn."

That was when Kate knew she was in trouble.

A man who would care for an elderly woman like that, a *shifter* who would care to that extent for an elderly, *human* woman, was absolutely someone she could fall in love with.

"So how's it going with you and Ryan?" she asked, a little desperate to think about anything other than how she might be falling in love with a panther.

"Not so great," Nick said to her surprise.

"Why? What happened?"

"I'm not really sure, but one minute we were flirting and the next he pitched headfirst into the engine he was working on."

"WHAT WERE YOU THINKING?" BYGUL BELLOWED at Soraya.

"I'm sorry," she said. "But you told us what Genghis Khat did to get the panther to kiss the bear. It worked for him!"

"Yes, but Genghis Khat's an earthbound cat which means he probably has better instincts than we do. Besides, it worked for him because the bear and panther were facing each other. The wolf you targeted was facing the car he was working on."

"It really wasn't the best of timing," Tivali said.

"I know." Soraya sighed. "The minute he fell and the Nick wolf didn't catch him, I knew I'd messed everything up. And now the Nick wolf's in the office and the Ryan wolf's sulking and they're not talking to each other. I may have completely ruined that romance, Tivali."

"Oh, don't worry, we'll fix it somehow."

"No!" Bygul exclaimed. "You'll not be fixing anything. Those two aren't the targets anyway. We need to focus on the panther and the bear!"

Kate gasped. "Is he all right?"

"Mostly, yeah. He has a little burn mark on his forehead, but he seems okay. Just embarrassed. He wouldn't look at me at all after that. I had to walk away to let his ego recover. You know how we wolves are."

"Oh, yeah."

"So anyway, hopefully he'll get over it. If not, well, that may have been the shortest romance on record."

"Oh, I'm sorry, Nick."

"Eh, it's fine. It's not like we're mates or anything, but that doesn't mean we couldn't enjoy a bit of flirtation and sexy times, right?"

"Absolutely. And who knows? Maybe you *are* mates and you just don't know it yet."

"Wolves aren't like bears, Kate. We usually know our mates right away."

She sighed. "I know."

The rest of the afternoon passed in a flurry of customers.

At a certain point, Jefferson dumped both Cleocatra and Genghis Khat into the office. "She's out of control today," he said to Kate. "Sorry, but we're knee-deep in oil pans and we just don't have time to keep an eye on her, and where she goes, Genghis Khat goes."

And so, Cleocatra spent the rest of the day in the office with them, wrestling air, pouncing on air, swiping at air and racing around and around the office before starting it all over again.

The day finally ended, with all of them exhausted and worn out.

Nick and Kate were sprawled in their chairs, having just checked out the last two customers, when Jefferson walked in the door.

"I take it back," Kate said. "You did need a receptionist. On Saturdays only, though."

Jefferson chuckled. "Well, thank you. This day was actually a lot easier than usual with the two of you here."

"Definitely," Ryan agreed, pushing in behind Jefferson. He headed for the Bear Necessities Station. "Need some fuel and coffee and then I'm headed home." He slid a glance Nick's way. "What are you up to this evening?"

Nick straightened in his chair. "I have no plans. You want to get dinner?"

Ryan grinned. "Absolutely."

"Awesome." Nick leapt to his feet, grabbed his jacket and said to Kate, "I'll see you Monday, boss."

"See you. Don't do anything I wouldn't."

Nick chuckled, grabbed Ryan by the arm and dragged him toward the door. "Don't worry. That leaves us an awful lot of wiggle room."

The door closed on the sound of Ryan's laughter.

"So how about you?" Kate asked Jefferson. "What are your plans for the evening?"

"I usually go to the Greensboro Diner for dinner. You want to join me?"

"Sure. What about the cats?"

"They're used to cats at the diner. Genghis Khat's a regular and Cleocatra's becoming one as well." He glanced down at Genghis Khat. "It's odd that Maggie never picked him up today."

"Does she know he's here?"

Jefferson's eyes widened. "I didn't call her. Did you?"

Kate shook her head.

Jefferson swung around and opened the door to the garage. "Yo, any of you guys call Maggie to let her know Genghis Khat was here?"

A chorus of negative responses made his shoulders slump.

"Damn."

Eight

BYGUL COULDN'T BELIEVE how completely undisciplined these cats were.

He'd spent the entire day trying to wrangle the cats, reign them in, convince Cleo to stop chasing them and begging Genghis Khat to do something, *anything*, to help.

By the end of the day, he was exhausted, and not convinced that anything had been accomplished or that any of the cats had learned anything at all.

In fact, he was pretty sure the only cat that learned a damn thing was Soraya and that was not to attack wolves who were working on a car's engine.

How that would help in any matchmaking scheme, he had no idea.

So basically, the entire day was a complete waste.

Not that he'd expected it to be anything else, considering the number of cats he was dragging along with him all day.

Then again, Jefferson and Kate left the garage together and she followed him all the way to Greensboro, so perhaps it wasn't a total waste.

As long as they kissed at the end of the evening, Bygul would consider this to be their first date.

A date he'd somehow managed to make happen despite being hampered by fifty-two useless cats all day long.

WHEN JEFFERSON WALKED INTO THE DINER, WITH Cleocatra on his shoulder, Genghis Khat in his arms, and Kate at his side, a cheer went up from the patrons.

"Does Maggie know you catnapped Genghis Khat again, Jefferson?" George called from the back of the diner.

Jefferson rolled his eyes. "I texted her, no worries."

"And what was her reaction?" Annie asked as she approached them with a couple menus. Normally she didn't bother, which told Jefferson that this was probably the first time Kate had dined there.

"Haven't heard back from her yet."

"Who's the bear?" Bud called from the kitchen.

Kate grinned. "Knock it off, Bud. Like you don't know who I am."

Jefferson's jaw dropped. "You know Bud?"

"We went to school together. So this is why you left

Worcester Falls." Kate crossed the diner to lean on the bar and chat with Bud through the window.

Jefferson followed, flabbergasted and a little annoyed the bear was stealing Kate's attention.

"Yep," Bud said. "Had a chance to open my own diner."

"I bet your parents were annoyed."

"Eh, they got over it. It wasn't like they were planning to retire anytime soon and I'm not one for taking orders."

"Yo, three triple cheeseburgers with the works," Annie called from across the room.

"On it!"

Kate grinned. "Yeah, I can see that. Well, it was good to see you."

"You too, Kate. Stop by before you leave."

She nodded, turned, grabbed Jefferson's hand and dragged him through the tables to an empty booth at the back of the diner.

The minute they reached the table, Genghis Khat lunged from Jefferson's arms, landed on the table and stretched out.

Kate rolled her eyes. "You weren't kidding when you said he was a regular here. Clearly, he's staked out his spot."

"Yep." Jefferson ushered Kate into the booth and settled across from her. "Pretty much everything here is to die for. You can't go wrong with anything on the menu."

"Oh, I'm sure of that, especially if Bud's doing the cooking. We bears are very particular about our food and he comes by his cooking talent naturally."

"I guess so. I never knew Bud grew up in Worcester Falls or that he had family there."

Before Kate could reply, Maggie arrived in the diner like a whirlwind. "You're a catnapping criminal, Jefferson Hewitt, and I'm done making excuses," she shouted from the doorway as stormed toward their table, dragging Jackson in her wake. When she reached them, she stopped, put her hands on her hips and demanded, "Jackson, arrest him!"

Jackson just shook his head and shoved his way into the booth, sitting beside Jefferson's date.

Jefferson scowled, but Jackson just grinned at him.

"So, who have we here?" He turned toward Kate, who was clearly flummoxed.

Jefferson had a moment of deja vu as he remembered how Maggie had studied the twins in just that same way, looking back and forth between them as if she were memorizing their features or searching for a difference.

She wouldn't find one, he knew, because they were truly identical. Most people wouldn't be able to tell them apart if it weren't for the fact that Jackson was usually in his sheriff's uniform and Jefferson typically had oil under his nails.

"I'm the Handsome Hewitt," Jefferson informed Kate, becoming a bit impatient with her scrutiny.

She chuckled. "Well, if you are, I hate to break it to you, but you probably share that title with this one here." She tilted her head toward Jackson, who grinned triumphantly.

"Nah. He's just the copy," Jefferson said. "*I'm* the Real McCat."

Jackson made a scoffing sound. "He's been saying that since we were kids, just because he was impatient and kicked his way out first. He thinks he's hilarious, but I'm not sure he understands the concept of identical twins."

Maggie and Kate both giggled.

"Move over, Jefferson." Maggie shoved his arm and he scooted over to make room for his sister-in-law. "Kate, you're sitting next to my mate, Jackson. Jackson, this is Kate Worcester."

"I'm completely intrigued right now," Jackson said. "You didn't tell me she was a bear, let alone a Worcester."

"I didn't know she was a bear when I hired her, and then, when I found out, I forgot to mention it. And what's a Worcester? You mean like the sauce?"

"That's Worcestershire sauce," Kate said.

"So, what's everyone eating?" Annie asked as she stepped up to the table.

"Oh, we're not staying," Maggie said.

"Hey, I'm hungry," Jackson exclaimed.

"We just came by to pick up Genghis Khat."

"And to give Jefferson a hard time. I owe him," Jackson said.

Maggie stood and scooped Genghis Khat up into her arms. "And you've given him that hard time and now we're leaving." She walked away without saying goodbye to any of them.

Jackson sighed. "I guess we're leaving. It was nice to meet you, Kate."

"You too."

Jefferson watched as Jackson caught up with Maggie and pulled her around.

He was relieved to see Maggie smiling at his brother, so she wasn't really annoyed. She'd just hit her limit for socializing, which Jefferson had learned could be pretty brief some days.

As the two walked out together, Maggie glanced over her shoulder and sent Jefferson a wink.

Holy hell.

She hadn't hit her limit at all. She'd clearly seen this meal for what it was and had done her part to protect it from her interfering, idiotic mate.

Jefferson grinned. "I owe Maggie big."

"What do you mean?" Kate asked.

"She just dragged Jackson out of here to give us time together."

Kate looked surprised. "Really?"

"Yep. So let's take advantage of it. Tell me everything."

As the hours passed, Kate found herself completely entranced by the panther.

He was funny and charming and full of humorous stories of what it was like growing up as part of a set.

He was interested in hearing about her own childhood and laughed at her stories of her overbearing, older brother who made dating practically impossible throughout her teens and twenties. She shared her underhanded methods for distracting him so that she could actually have a life, including on one memorable occasion, sprinkling itching powder all over his bed.

He'd been so miserable, he had no idea his little sister had sneaked out of the house for a school dance. That was the night she'd lost her virginity, she confided, and Mason hadn't a clue.

She got better at the subterfuge the older she got and things got way better once she moved out on her own, but Mason was still overbearing and controlling and she'd learned to mostly live with it, except for those rare occasions when it interfered with her job.

The hours slid by slowly as Kate and Jefferson laughed and talked. They were the last customers in the diner when they finally left as it was closing.

Cleocatra had made her presence known many times throughout the evening, demanding Jefferson's attention.

Somehow he'd managed to kiss her, pet her and adore her all while keeping his focus on Kate.

She found that to be incredibly sexy, that he could soothe Cleocatra and make her feel so important, all the while never taking his eyes off Kate and never making her feel as if he'd chosen the kitten over her.

He'd make an incredible father, she realized, for he also

never made Cleocatra feel as if he'd chosen Kate over the kitten.

Jefferson walked her to where their cars were parked. He settled Cleocatra inside his car, then turned and backed Kate up against hers. He captured her lips in a searing kiss and long moments went by in a heartbeat.

Kate lost herself in the heat of the moment.

Shivers ran up and down her spine and if Bud hadn't driven by and honked his car in farewell at that very moment, she might have climbed Jefferson like a tree and taken him against the hood of one of their cars.

They broke apart and stood there panting, staring at each other, wanting.

Kate caught movement in the car behind him, but couldn't really see what was going on.

It was probably Cleocatra, blending in with the dark night, spying on them.

Yep. Definitely Cleocatra.

Kate could see just her eyes, glaring out at them from the side window.

She giggled.

Jefferson turned and let out a bark of laughter. "Guess that means it's time for us to go." He turned and swept Kate into his arms again, for one last kiss. When he set her back down, her knees were wobbly.

He helped her into her car, then watched as she pulled away.

The entire way home, she was tempted to turn right back around and go to his place. She knew his address because they'd made plans to meet there tomorrow. They were planning to spend the day together and she couldn't wait.

Nine

THE DATE THE night before had ended in kisses, which meant the romance was progressing nicely.

Except for one thing.

Cleocatra.

The kitten continued to be a problem.

Jefferson was pretty good at paying attention to her most of the time, but the minute he had to do something like work on a car, or was focused on kissing Kate, Cleocatra went nuts.

She definitely did *not* like sharing her human companion with anyone else.

Bygul had no idea how to convince her to accept Kate's presence in their lives.

Even worse, Jefferson wasn't his only client. Bygul had a long list of matches still to be made and several were reaching a critical stage where his presence was absolutely necessary to ensure success.

He had no choice but to focus his attentions on these other matches and hope things didn't fall apart in his absence.

This was probably a futile hope, considering Jefferson had invited Kate to his house.

His house, where Cleo lived, a dwelling he was certain she considered to be all her territory.

Jefferson had invited another woman into Cleo's territory and Bygul did not predict good things would come from this scenario.

He could only hope that Cleo didn't ruin everything.

"Bygul, Bygul." Tivali raced across the lawn of PPM, headed straight for him.

Great.

What on earth did she want now?

"Don't worry, brother. She has a fabulous idea to help you."

Bygul jumped. He hated it when his brother, Kalyn, sneaked up on him like that, and he absolutely had zero trust that Kalyn would recognize a good idea if it bit him on the tail.

"I'm so glad I caught you, Bygul." Tivali skidded to a stop in front of him, Soraya at her side.

Even worse.

Soraya was apparently involved.

"We know you have so many matches on your plate and

you probably don't have time to monitor Jefferson and the bear today, so we thought we'd offer to take care of that for you."

"Take care of what?"

"Monitoring the panther and bear, of course. We know this match is at a very sensitive moment and delicacy is everything."

Delicacy. Right. Because they'd shown so much of that when trying to match the wolves the day before.

"We'll take care of everything, brother," Kalyn said. "You have no need to worry at all."

Bygul glared at his brother.

He had no doubt the other two had roped Kalyn into this idiotic plan because they assumed Bygul wouldn't say no to his own brother.

Well, they were wrong!

Of course, he'd—

"I'm really looking forward to this opportunity to help you with one of your matches since you were so helpful with one of mine last month," Kalyn said.

Bygul froze.

Dear goddess of all matches everywhere.

He'd completely forgotten that disaster!

Blocked it from his mind, more like.

In front of others, Kalyn pretended that Bygul had helped him out with that horror show, but the two brothers knew the truth.

In fact, Bygul had made a terrible situation that much worse.

Which meant he definitely owed Kalyn a tremendous favor.

Too bad Jefferson and the bear would have to be the ones to pay that price.

When Jefferson had first realized the bear was probably his mate, he'd panicked a little.

A panther with a bear just didn't seem a good idea.

And him with this particular bear seemed completely outrageous.

She scared his panther, made him whimper just a little.

It took a while for Jefferson to realize his panther actually enjoyed the sensation of being a tiny bit scared of their mate.

In fact, he seemed to get off on it.

Once Jefferson realized that, and once they'd kissed once or twice or a couple hundred times, he was all in.

The woman was sexy as hell and she lit every single one of his nerves on fire when she touched him.

He couldn't ask for more in a mate, not really.

So she intimidated him a little.

He imagined that would simply result in sexy times being that much sexier.

The only hitch in the entire situation was Cleocatra.

She didn't seem all that fond of Kate.

Not that Kate seemed to mind.

Oh, she'd roared when startled, and on one memorable occasion, had even shrieked, but mostly she just tolerated it with a tiny smirk on her face.

Like when Cleocatra was attached to her head the day before.

Kate had given up her attempts to remove the kitten's claws fairly quickly and instead had seemed amused by the entire situation.

He knew he was.

So maybe it wasn't that big a deal, after all.

Except he wanted Cleocatra happy, not stressed out.

With this in mind, he tried to prepare the kitten for the arrival of their guest.

He talked to her about the bear and how much Kate liked Cleocatra (a bit of an exaggeration, to be sure, but he was certain she was headed that way) and how lucky Cleocatra was to have two shifters who absolutely adored her.

Cleocatra had seemed to perk up when he mentioned having two shifters, so he was mildly optimistic that today might not be a total disaster.

KATE ARRIVED WITH THREE BEAR-SIZED PICNIC baskets.

She'd debated only bringing one, but there was no way just one basket would fill her bear and then she'd end up forcing the panther to feed her every morsel he had in the house, which to her seemed a bit rude.

Sure, showing up with three picnic baskets meant he'd clue in, if he hadn't already, to Kate's ravenous appetite.

It wasn't a fact she'd ever had to worry about when dating other bears.

She'd had to completely hide it from the one human she'd dated and she typically didn't reveal her full appetite to non-bear shifters until at least the fifth or sixth date.

However, if her suspicions were true and this panther really was her mate, he would need to know what he was getting into and she would need to know if he couldn't handle it, so they could both run away if need be.

Therefore, hiding her bearish nature just didn't seem like a good idea.

Besides, the truth was going to come out no later than tomorrow anyway, because that's when he'd discover the latest renovations at the garage.

She'd stopped by there on her way to his house and found everything progressing nicely. She had high hopes she'd be cooking in their office kitchen no later than tomorrow morning.

Hopefully Jefferson wouldn't be too terribly upset, especially since it would mean more scrumptious pastries all day long, but if he was, oh well.

He did sign the rental agreement, after all.

Of course, if she'd been his attorney, she would never have advised him to sign it.

He gave away entirely too much control of a good portion of his garage space in that agreement, not that he seemed to care.

Of course, if she'd been a good employee, she would have advised him to consult an attorney, but that wouldn't have been in her best interests, so she didn't.

And now they'd just have to deal with the consequences. He with a full-fledged kitchen in his garage and she with his temper if he wasn't pleased.

First, though, she was going to enjoy Snack Through Sunday by going on a hike and a picnic with the sexiest panther in existence and by eating through the contents of three bear-sized picnic baskets.

To Kate's surprise, Cleocatra seemed quite happy to see her when she first arrived.

The kitten bounced over to her and stretched up on her hind legs.

Kate leaned down to pick her up and wasn't quite fast enough to avoid the snap of Cleo's teeth.

"Seriously?" Kate slid a hand beneath the kitten's

bottom and lifted. Her teeth were wrapped around one of Kate's fingers and she was letting out tiny, adorable growls as she tried to chew through Kate's admittedly tough hide.

Even in her human form, Kate's skin wasn't easily dented.

"What is she doing?" Jefferson chuckled.

"Apparently she thinks my finger is a chew toy."

"Now, Cleocatra, come here, darling." Jefferson worked to detach Cleo from Kate's finger and for a moment, Kate thought he wouldn't be successful and she'd be stuck with a kitten hanging from her finger for the rest of her life, but then with one final adorable growl, Cleo let go.

Jefferson cuddled her to his chest, and with laughter clear in his voice, said, "Sorry about that," then leaned in close and caught Kate's lips with his own.

Kate forgot the kitten and everything else in the heat of his kiss. She stepped forward, needing to get closer, to feel his chest against hers, to—

"Ow!" Kate jerked away and slapped a hand to her left breast. "Ow, you little demon cat. I think she bit my nipple!"

"Sorry," Jefferson choked out. "I'll set her down now."

"Yeah, yeah." Kate pulled her tee-shirt out and stared at it. "See those tiny holes?" She smoothed her shirt back down and stared at her breast.

Yep. Those little puncture marks framed her nipple exactly.

Little beast.

She glared down at Cleocatra, who was clearly feeling no

remorse as she ran around the room in happy, darting sprints.

"Would you like me to examine your nipple?" Jefferson offered in a much-too-serious voice. "I'd be happy to blow on it, to soothe it with my tongue and to stroke it better, if you'd like."

Kate tried to maintain her composure, but really he was too much. "Oh, you would, would you?" She burst into laughter. "You're incorrigible."

He grinned. "That's me. Ready to go on a hike? Or would you rather stay here and have me provide a bit of nipple relief?"

Kate snickered. Though she thought she'd probably enjoy his brand of nipple relief, she decided it would be smarter to go on that hike. Besides, she was hungry. "I vote for hiking."

Jefferson shook his head in mock disappointment. "You have no idea what you're missing, but let's go then."

He led her across the field at the back of his house and into the woods that stretched from his town all the way to Worcester Falls.

She wondered how often they'd both been inside these woods at the same time, miles from each other, with no idea the other even existed.

They each carried one of the picnic baskets Kate had brought and stopped often for some Bear Necessities.

"You know," Jefferson said on their first stop. "I believe

kisses should be included among these Bear Necessities we can't live without. What do you think?"

Kate grinned and crawled across the blanket they were sitting on to straddle his lap. "I think you may have a point. We should test this out and see."

And so the kissing began.

Every break, every pause even became punctuated with kisses that raised the heat level between them to almost unbearable degrees.

By the time they reached the waterfall Jefferson had chosen as the site for their picnic lunch, Kate was practically panting with desire.

They'd barely set the picnic baskets down before she was on Jefferson and the two of them were on the ground.

They rolled around and kissed and indulged in more heavy petting before breaking for lunch.

"We'll need the energy," Kate pointed out.

Jefferson just nodded in agreement and they set about pulling out the lunch Kate had prepared.

They spent hours at the waterfall, consuming everything left inside both picnic baskets. Well, Kate ate most of it, but Jefferson ate his fair share and as the day wore on, he made eating a truly erotic experience as he fed her little morsels and followed it up with devastating kisses.

By the time they made it back to his house (because Jefferson insisted he wasn't going to take her for the first time on the hard ground—"I have at least that much self-control," he proclaimed loftily), Kate was a mass of hormones, just waiting to explode.

Then they walked in the front door.

CLEOCATRA WAS *NOT* HAPPY HER HUMAN HAD gone off with the bear, leaving her behind. She was even more annoyed when Bygul didn't show up to transport her to Jefferson.

He sent in three substitute cats instead and even put together, they weren't as smart as Bygul.

Cleocatra had met Tivali and Soraya already, but the one named Kalyn she'd never met before. He looked a lot like Bygul, except he didn't sound like him at all.

Not as bossy.

Or as smart.

The minute they arrived, Cleocatra demanded they take her to Jefferson, so they transported her to the garage, but Jefferson wasn't there.

Instead, there were all kinds of people wandering in and out, banging on things and tearing down walls and basically destroying the place.

Cleocatra couldn't believe it!

Jefferson would be so angry when he returned.

They also messed with her stuff. She had a litter box in

the bathroom and another one in the back storage room and both of those rooms were being destroyed!

This was a disaster.

Cleocatra wanted to stay and protect the place from the destroyers, but she also missed Jefferson and hated that he was with the bear without her.

So she demanded once again that the cats take her to Jefferson.

The problem was they didn't seem to know where he was, so they ended up popping in and out of various places like the diner and a place called a barbershop and Maggie's place where they saw Genghis Khat and Maggie and even Jackson, but no Jefferson.

After spying on the three of them for a moment—Cleocatra was surprised Genghis Khat didn't seem upset when Jackson kissed Maggie, and in fact, when the kiss was over, had nudged Jackson's hand and got some pets in return—they all returned to Jefferson's house.

"I have no idea where they are," Tivali said. "And this is exhausting, popping in and out all over the place."

"Agreed," Soraya said.

Cleocatra flopped down and placed her head on her paws. Her human was out there somewhere without her and the bear could be eating him right now and she wasn't there to protect him.

What if he never came home?

What if she was left all alone again, without Jefferson by her side?

"Oh, sweetheart, don't be sad." Tivali dropped down beside her and began grooming her. "Everything's going to be just fine. They'll be home soon and he'll give you lots of attention."

"Absolutely," Soraya said.

Or he'd have so much fun with the bear that he'd completely forget about Cleo and not pay her any attention at all.

"I doubt that will happen," Kalyn said. "Bygul says he absolutely adores you."

"Exactly," Tivali said.

"I've got an idea," Soraya said. "Let's have some fun. We can play a few games. What do you guys say?"

"What a wonderful idea," Tivali said. "You'll be cheered up in no time, Cleocatra."

So that was how they ended up racing around the room, playing with anything that remotely resembled a cat toy and when Cleocatra recognized the scent of the giant basket sitting on the floor in the entryway, they had a ball shredding it with their claws.

JEFFERSON AND KATE STUMBLED INTO THE HOUSE late that afternoon, frantically kissing each other and were seconds from tearing each other's clothes off when a yowl from Cleocatra had them pulling away from each other, just in time for Jefferson to catch the kitten as she leapt straight up into his arms.

Cleocatra's fur was on end and she was clearly agitated. She hissed at Kate and swiped at her with both front paws, claws extended.

If Jefferson hadn't had a good hold on her, she would have completely overbalanced herself what with the reach of those swipes, especially when they came one right after the other, right paw, then left, then right again.

"It's okay, Cleocatra," Kate crooned, but Cleocatra was clearly not interested in being soothed.

Jefferson cuddled her close to his chest and murmured, "What's the matter, sweet love?"

She let out a distressed meow and buried her face in his neck.

"Holy hell," Kate muttered.

Jefferson glanced up, saw she was staring into the living room and turned to get a good look.

"Damn."

A side table had been knocked over and the lamp that had been on it had rolled across the floor.

At one time, his coffee table had sported a couple auto mechanic magazines, several remotes, a couple bills and some junk mail. None of those items were on the coffee table any longer. It was completely cleared off and scattered throughout the living room were the remnants of those bills and magazines and junk mail.

Jefferson could see what he thought might be the light bill sticking out from under the couch while shreds from the magazines were pretty much everywhere.

It also looked like Cleo had somehow managed to get onto the shelf where he kept the basket of cat toys because the entire basket was on the floor and toys were scattered everywhere.

In addition—"I think she found the third picnic basket. Doesn't look like she got inside it though."

Kate snickered. "It's pretty much bear–proof, so I'm not surprised. She shredded the outer layer pretty good, though. Is this the first time you've left her alone?"

"Pretty much, yeah. I mean, I leave her alone every morning, but you know how that goes, which means this is the first time she's been alone for any length of time, considering she didn't join us when we were hiking like she does when I'm at the garage."

"Which is probably a good thing. The woods aren't the safest spot for a kitten, but I'm thinking she didn't appreciate being left behind."

"Yeah." Jefferson sighed. "This is a disaster."

Cleo let out a soft meow and nuzzled the underside of his jaw.

"Oh, now you want to play nice, huh? Well, unfortunately, I'm going to have to clean things up, so there won't be any playing for a while." He went to set her on the ground, but she stiffened in his hands and let out a yowl.

Jefferson winced, pulled the kitten close again and glanced at Kate helplessly.

Kate grinned. "I'll clean. You soothe the beast."

"You don't have to do that."

"Of course, I don't, but it's the least I can do since you left her alone because of me."

Jefferson settled on the couch with Cleocatra and focused on petting her and soothing her temper away.

Cleocatra cuddled close, but no matter what he did, she wouldn't start purring, and in fact, kept her eyes open and trained on Kate the entire time, no matter where Kate was in the room.

Kate bustled around picking up cat toys, sweeping up remnants of paper and returning items to wherever they'd fallen from.

Once the basket of toys was mostly full, she carried it to the couch and settled it next to Jefferson.

Cleocatra glared at Kate balefully and let out a tiny hiss of warning.

Kate chuckled. "Yes, I know. He's your human, but do you think I could maybe borrow him for just a moment?" Kate leaned forward as if to kiss Jefferson and Cleocatra let loose with a series of hissing snarls.

Kate laughed and pulled back. "All right, guess not. Well, Jefferson, I think maybe I should let you and Cleocatra have the evening to yourselves. You know, repair that bond of yours."

Jefferson groaned. "I'm so sorry." He should have said to

hell with his self-control and taken her in the woods. Now he'd be taking cold showers all night instead.

Kate giggled. "It's okay. We'll work on it."

Jefferson stood and followed her to the door, cradling Cleocatra in his arm furthest from Kate.

Kate opened the door and stepped out onto the porch.

Jefferson stepped out after her, turned and set Cleocatra down in the entryway, then quickly closed the screen door, trapping the kitten inside the house.

He turned and pulled Kate into his arms. "One more kiss for the road," he murmured against her lips before pouring all of his passion into the kiss.

IT WAS MONDAY.

Bygul's least favorite day of the week.

In his experience, humans were less cooperative, more stubborn and far crankier on Mondays than any other day of the week.

After listening to Kalyn's report from the day before, Bygul was feeling quite cranky himself.

Apparently, they'd been unsuccessful in tracking down Jefferson and the bear the day before, which meant they were unable to monitor that romance.

However, according to Kalyn, things had been looking quite promising when the two stumbled into the house, clearly on the road toward a passionate mating.

Unfortunately, Cleo had her own mission.

And it apparently was to keep that mating from ever happening.

Per Kalyn, the bear had gone home alone and Jefferson had gone to bed with only Cleo for company.

Based on this information, Bygul decided it was time to leave Cleo out of all plans because she was obviously trying to sabotage their mate matching efforts.

Therefore, he skipped right over Jefferson's house and went straight to Maggie's that morning where he picked up Genghis Khat, who informed him it was about time he left Cleo behind.

Bygul figured G.K. was simply tired of the kitten chasing his tail all the time.

He transported the two of them to the garage, then said to G.K., "Look, I have to get back to teach my class. Just do everything you can to get the bear and the panther together before Maggie comes storming in and takes you back home. Maybe without Cleo around, this romance will finally start moving forward."

SEEING AS CLEOCATRA ALWAYS ENDED UP AT THE garage anyway, that morning, Jefferson just took her with him.

He figured he might as well, especially since he didn't want to leave her for even the short amount of time it would take him to drive to the garage, given how upset she'd been the night before.

The minute he arrived at the garage, he knew something weird was going on.

Ryan and Pete had already arrived, but were standing just inside the garage door, staring.

"What's going on?" Jefferson nudged Ryan forward. "Why aren't we moving?"

"Uh," was Ryan's only response before he stepped to one side and Lyle to the other, so that Jefferson could move into the building.

Once he was inside, he knew exactly why the other mechanics were acting so weird.

At some point in the last thirty-six hours, the entrance had been transformed.

The garage had four bays with four garage doors that lifted. To the left of those garage doors was the single door they'd just entered. That door usually led into a largely unused garage space that was about two times the size of one of the bays.

The back half of the space was taken up by the office and storage room.

There were two stairs leading up to the office and to the left of those stairs had been a very small bathroom.

Jefferson had considered setting up a lobby area in the unused space that led up to the office, but had eventually decided he didn't want to encourage customers to hang around while they were working, and so he'd just left it as is.

About half that empty space was now gone. A wall had been built directly to the left of where they now stood, running from the door to the stairs and ending where the original bathroom had once stood.

The new wall had two doors labeled "Mechanics" and "Customers and Office Personnel."

The hiss of annoyance he let out startled Cleocatra whose claws came out and prickled his skin a little.

Jefferson dropped a kiss on her head. "Sorry, little one. Let's go check out the craziness." He walked over to the first door and flung it open.

His jaw dropped.

"Wow," Ryan said from behind him.

"Didn't expect that," Lyle said.

"What's going on?" Pete walked up behind them.

Jefferson didn't reply, just walked slowly into the new restroom that had clearly been built with them in mind.

The room was split in two. The area he walked into was a carpeted lounge, with two leather armchairs, a table with flowers and—Jefferson looked closer—yes, the exact magazines he'd had on his coffee table that Cleocatra had shredded the day before.

To the right was an open doorway that led into a tiled bathroom with a couple stalls and urinals.

"You should check this out!" Lyle exclaimed from inside the tiled room. "There's a pumice stone in here and nail brushes and lotions and wow—this is some high-end, expensive mechanics' soap."

"Damn," Pete said from the lounge area. "I'm spending my breaks in here from now on."

Jefferson just shook his head and walked out.

Cleocatra meowed at him.

"It's okay, baby." He dropped a kiss on her nose and scratched her under the chin.

She purred in response.

He wanted to be mad, but really how could he? He'd signed the agreement, after all, and Kate had warned him. It's just that when nothing happened, he'd assumed she'd changed her mind.

Obviously, she hadn't. There was no way he could complain, though, not when the bathroom had clearly been created with his comfort in mind.

Curious now, he wandered next door into the other restroom.

The setup was exactly the same, but in reverse with the lounging area on the right and the tiled bathroom to the left.

Just like next door, there were two leather armchairs and a table sporting flowers and magazines (though these appeared to be focused on news and entertainment).

The bathroom looked similar as well, with three stalls and a variety of lotions and soaps and nail care utensils.

What impressed him the most was that neither bathroom was nicer than the other. Usually, men were thought to not need the special fancy additions that were so common in women's restrooms.

He also liked that the doors weren't labeled according to

gender, but instead according to roles, which made sense considering the accessories in each.

Jefferson stepped out into the garage, just as Lyle exclaimed, "Hey, there's a third door back here!"

There was indeed. It was right at the base of the stairs, where the original bathroom had once stood.

Jefferson hadn't noticed it before because it didn't have a sign like the other two.

Except, now that Jefferson looked closer, he realized it did have one; it was just much lower to the ground.

He let out a bark of laughter.

The door was full-sized, but it sported a pet door at the bottom and above the pet door was a sign that featured a black cat.

Grinning, he opened the door and discovered inside a cat bathroom about half the size of the human ones, but with many of the same features. The area was split in two just like in the other rooms, with one half being carpeted and the other half tile.

In the carpeted area, there was a single armchair—not leather, but instead patterned in cats at play—a couple cat beds and a basket of toys that Jefferson noted included many of the same toys Cleocatra loved playing with at the house.

The tiled area to the right had two covered litter boxes (both decorated with cat images) on either side of a sink which had a tiny trash can in the shape of a cat sitting on its countertop.

There was also a cabinet with cat-shaped doorknobs

standing against the wall across from the sink and litter boxes. A quick peek inside revealed bags of litter, a litter scoop and a box of trash bags.

Jefferson was literally speechless.

She'd created an entire bathroom just for Cleocatra.

The kitten who had made it clear she didn't like Kate.

Jefferson walked back out into the cat lounge area and murmured to Cleocatra, "Look at all the toys she bought for you." He set her down in front of the basket and watched as she sniffed it and the toys inside it, then sniffed around the chair, then investigated both cat beds, before heading back to the basket of toys.

She climbed into the basket and batted a ball out, then followed it onto the floor where she sent it skittering across the room, then chased after it.

Jefferson waited a few moments and when he was certain she was fully entertained and wouldn't even notice when he left, he sneaked out the door, letting it close behind him.

He glanced around and found only Pete waiting.

He raised an eyebrow.

"They went upstairs for coffee and snacks and to see if there were any other changes."

Jefferson sighed. "Well, we might as well endure all the shocks at once. Let's go, then."

They walked up the two stairs into the office.

The first thing Jefferson noticed was the door to the storage unit had been moved further down the wall from where it had originally stood, and was now a swinging door.

The wall it was on had been completely rebuilt and looked quite natural, blending into the rest of the walls of the office, as if it had never been torn down.

He wasn't at all surprised to see Lyle at the Bear Necessities Station, clearly perusing the day's offerings, while Ryan was leaning against Nick's desk, flirting with him.

Ryan insisted they weren't mates, that they were just having a bit of fun, but Jefferson wouldn't be at all surprised if he was wrong about that.

"Where's Kate?" Jefferson asked as Pete made a beeline for the food.

Nick waved a hand behind him toward the swinging doors and said, "Kitchen," without taking his eyes off Ryan.

Jefferson was already walking toward the swinging doors when the word "kitchen" registered. He shook his head, convinced he couldn't have heard right, then shoved his way into the former storage room to discover that yes, he had indeed heard correctly.

The storage room had been completely transformed into what looked to be an industrial kitchen, with high-end appliances and a large island in the middle. The only thing that appeared to have remained the same from before was the wall to the right, which was still covered with the original shelves that had been part of the storage room, which were now clearly being used to house every ingredient known to man or shifter.

He really shouldn't be surprised.

The way Kate (and apparently all bears) ate, having a

kitchen and full pantry available twenty-four seven was probably a matter of survival.

Just one more of those Bear Necessities.

And speaking of Kate, she stood with her back to Jefferson and was in the process of transferring cookies to a cooling rack she'd set up on the island.

Jefferson waited until she'd finished and had set the hot tray aside before saying her name.

She whirled and smiled. "Jefferson!"

KATE DIDN'T WANT TO ADMIT IT, BUT SHE WAS nervous.

Super nervous.

After leaving Jefferson's place the night before, she'd stopped at the garage again, to check on the progress, and had been thrilled at the results.

The workers had just been finishing up and the foreman had given her a tour.

It was incredible.

Everything had worked out.

Even the furniture had been delivered on time.

She'd been especially thrilled with the cat room.

Not that the little demon deserved it or anything.

Still, she'd gone out the night before and made some extra purchases for a few final touches.

She'd picked up the magazines she'd seen on Jefferson's coffee table and some of Cleocatra's favorite cat toys.

Vases of flowers for the bathrooms, which was really quite ridiculous, and of course, a huge grocery run for everything she needed to be able to bake at a moment's notice.

She'd arrived home with a full SUV and a whole pile of nerves.

Shopping had helped to settle her raging hormones, but had done nothing for the nerves.

She'd slept very poorly the night before, thoughts on Jefferson the entire time, imagining how the night might have ended if it weren't for the demon cat and worrying about his reaction to the bathrooms and the kitchen.

She'd given up on sleeping around four in the morning and had decided to go ahead and come in and begin the day early.

She'd been baking since just after five and it had gone a long way toward calming her down. Well, that and being able to snack as she baked.

As long as she focused on the baking (and the eating) and kept her thoughts away from Jefferson, she thought she should be able to keep the nerves at bay.

Of course, that was easier said than done, but she did her best.

Then, in the midst of all that baking and eating, Jefferson arrived.

The minute she heard his voice, all her nerves just flew away.

She whirled with a grin, exclaimed his name and hurried across the kitchen to hurl herself into his arms.

Jefferson caught her close, settled one hand at the base of her neck and slid another down her back to cup her ass and lift her.

Kate wrapped her legs around his waist and kissed him.

Or maybe he kissed her.

Either way, their lips were melded together, tongues twining deep with tingles spreading all over her body as heat blanketed her in waves.

Jefferson carried her a few steps further into the kitchen and then she was on the kitchen island and he was between her legs and they were devouring each other with no end in sight.

Kate heard Nick yelling, "Yo, Kate, you've got a visitor!"

She could tell from the tone that he was trying to warn her about something. The words should mean something, but all she could do and feel was Jefferson.

His lips, his hard cock right against the part of her that ached for him, his hands on her back, on her neck, slipping beneath her pants to cup her ass, and then there was a horrendous roar that rattled every pot in the kitchen and Jefferson was gone.

Kate was left all alone, swaying in place on the kitchen island, so close to climax, it actually hurt for it to be yanked away.

She heard the sound of another roar—a roar she recognized—and then a huge crash.

Oh, shit!

She leapt down from the island, hurtled through the swinging doors and came to a screeching halt.

The first thing she noticed was Nick cowering under his desk.

She sent him a demanding look and he pointed to the windows overlooking the garage.

One was completely shattered with Mason standing in front of it, glaring down into the shop,

"Mason!" Kate shrieked. "What the hell is wrong with you?"

She raced out the door, leapt down the steps into the garage and hurried to Jefferson's side, falling to her knees beside him.

He'd landed flat on his back, but was struggling up onto his elbows when she reached him.

"What happened?" He seemed disoriented and had several cuts from the glass, but mostly looked okay.

"My idiot brother tossed you through the window."

Jefferson chuckled. "I'm pretty sure you assured me that wouldn't happen."

"No, I just said he rarely caused permanent damage." Not that that made it any better or anything. She was seriously going to kill her brother.

"Kate, stop fussing over that panther and get your ass in here," Mason bellowed through the shattered window.

"Excuse me?" Kate leapt to her feet and stormed back up the stairs into the office.

Mason disappeared from the window as he turned to face his angry sister.

"PSST. RYAN!"

Jefferson looked up and watched, a bit stunned, as Nick passed several things through the now broken window to Ryan.

"You okay, boss?" Lyle asked.

Jefferson nodded. "Survived a bear attack. I think I'm pretty good."

Nick hopped through the window, then grinned down at Jefferson. "Man, you're better than good if you can stand after an encounter with Mason Worcester. Let's see how you do." He reached out a hand, Jefferson grasped it and allowed the wolf to pull him to his feet.

Jefferson shook out his hands and arms and looked up toward the office, where Mason and Kate were still roaring at each other.

"Should I try to intervene?"

"Nah," Nick said. "Mason would never hurt Kate, but this'll probably go on for a while." He turned to the other wolves. "We might as well get comfortable and enjoy the show. It's Munch Away Monday so I brought popcorn and pastries."

So that's what he'd been passing through the window to Ryan.

At that moment, Cleocatra came bolting through the pet door and raced across the concrete toward Jefferson.

"What's the matter, baby?" Jefferson scooped her into his arms and cuddled her close. "Is the roaring too loud for you? They're just bears, sweetie. You can't expect them to be quiet."

A few moments later, once he was done soothing Cleocatra, he noticed the wolves had taken the opportunity to somehow locate his set of collapsible chairs and had arranged them in a row facing the office windows.

Inside, you could see Kate pacing back and forth, arms waving, while Mason stood back, arms crossed, glowering. Both bears were roaring at the top of their lungs, making it hard to understand anything they were saying.

The wolves were all eating popcorn while keeping up a running commentary.

"He's pretty intimidating," Lyle observed.

"Yeah, but so is she," Nick said.

"Who do you think's going to win this argument?" Ryan asked.

"I'm betting on Kate myself," Nick said.

"Fifty on the brother," Pete said.

"I'll take that bet," Nick said.

Jefferson shook his head and rolled his eyes. "You know,

there is work to be done around here. Car repairs, oil changes, ring a bell?"

Ryan looked at Jefferson, then back at the shouting bears. "I hate to say it, but I'm pretty sure our boss is doomed."

"No shit," Pete said.

"There's no way he'll ever win an argument against that," Lyle said with a wave of the hand toward the raging Kate.

"Yeah, she is kind of scary when in a rage," Nick said.

"Glad it's not me," Pete said cheerfully.

They all looked at Jefferson, who just glared back at them.

"Dude, that grizzly kicked your ass," Pete said.

"Well, you can't blame the grizzly," Ryan said. "I mean, Jefferson *was* fooling around with his sister."

"Yeah, but Jefferson didn't even get one punch in," Pete protested.

"True, but it's not every day you get attacked by a giant grizzly," Lyle pointed out.

"He wasn't even in his bear form," Pete said. "You'd think Jefferson could have at least fought back a little, not just gone belly up."

"Hey, he ambushed me," Jefferson defended himself. "One minute I'm kissing Kate, the next I'm flying through the window."

"You mean to tell me you didn't smell that grizzly coming?" Pete exclaimed.

"All I could smell was Kate," Jefferson said morosely.

"YOU NEED TO COME BACK TO WORK!" MASON roared at Kate.

"I *am* at work and I'm doing all the work I used to do, but in a new location and one where I don't have to deal with your controlling nature on a daily basis."

"Well, who can blame me when the second my back is turned, you're fraternizing with wolves and kissing panthers!"

"He's my mate!" Kate roared.

Dead silence.

"Say it isn't so, Kate," Mason shouted.

She shrugged. "Well, I haven't let my bear out yet, so I'm not positive, but considering my bear wants to get closer and to roll in his scent, rather than tear him limb from limb, I'm pretty damn sure we're mates."

"You've broken my heart, Kate."

"Why? Because he's not a bear?"

"No. Because he doesn't live in Worcester Falls."

"Oh for heaven's sake, he lives in Greensboro. It's a forty minute drive tops."

"Harumph. Whatever. Introduce me to this panther of yours."

Kate let out a huff. "Fine. Let's go." She stamped out the door and down the stairs into the garage, where for some reason, the wolves were all sitting in chairs she associated with outdoor events.

She grinned at the sight of Nick and Ryan, leaning toward each other, sharing a bucket of popcorn, clearly into each other in a massive way.

Jefferson was the only one not eating popcorn *or* sitting down. Instead, he was standing off to the side, cradling Cleocatra in his arms, and glaring at the wolves.

"Jefferson," Kate said, drawing his attention to her. "This is my idiot brother, Mason." She waved a hand behind her.

Mason glared at Jefferson, who just glared back.

"Mason's sorry for overreacting," Kate said, sending an elbow into her brother's gut.

He grunted, then held out his hand to Jefferson.

After a brief hesitation, Jefferson reached out and accepted the handshake.

From the wince on Jefferson's face, Kate was pretty sure Mason was trying to grind his bones into dust. "Knock it off, Mason." She slammed her elbow into his side again, then slid under Jefferson's arm to stand at his side and glare at her brother.

Mason scowled, but relented.

Jefferson reclaimed his hand and discreetly flexed it.

"You're coming to dinner Wednesday night," Mason said to Kate, "and you're bringing the panther with you."

Kate sighed. "Fine. Whatever. Just go. We have a business to run here."

Mason gave her a look that clearly expressed his disdain for that business, then turned and walked out.

"Nice fellow," Lyle said.

"Sorry, guys. I would have introduced you, but then you'd have been subjected to The Mason Handshake of Doom like Jefferson here and I thought I'd spare you that. At least for now."

"And we appreciate it," Pete said.

"Most definitely," Ryan agreed. "I'll be needing my hands later." He waggled his brows suggestively at Nick, who snorted in amusement.

"So." Jefferson turned to Kate, a huge grin on his face. "I hear that I'm your mate."

Eleven

WHEN BYGUL POPPED back into the garage after his class was over, he was dismayed to find complete and utter chaos waiting for him.

What had he said about Mondays again?

Oh, right.

They were an absolute nightmare.

First of all, he saw immediately that Cleo was in Jefferson's arms and he had no idea how that had happened.

He'd deliberately left her behind today!

The next thing he noticed was that Genghis Khat was stretched out in the middle of the floor, apparently taking a nap.

What kind of matchmaking cat was he?

The third thing he noticed was that Jefferson was

standing with all the wolves and Kate was nowhere to be seen.

So, apparently G.K. was not only napping on the job, but not even doing the bare minimum to ensure the panther and the bear spent time together.

The fourth thing he noticed were the very loud roars coming from the office.

Okay, maybe that was the first thing he noticed, but it certainly wasn't the most important.

Although it did prove his point about Mondays: humans were less cooperative, more stubborn and far *crankier* those days of the week.

It was at that moment, Kate's voice roared out louder than every other sound in the place, including that of the other bear, "He's my mate!"

Dead silence followed.

Bygul happened to be staring at Jefferson right at that very moment, so he saw the look of pure joy that crossed the panther's face before he quickly schooled his features back into a neutral expression.

Perhaps G.K. hadn't abandoned the mission after all. In fact, if the smirk on his face was any indication, the cat was definitely taking credit for this turn of events.

Cleo, on the other hand, looked quite worried.

Bygul made his way over to her. "Don't worry, Cleo," he started to say, but then realized Jefferson was already taking care of it.

"No worries, my sweet little Cleocatra," Jefferson

murmured into her ear. "She may be my mate, but you'll always be my precious baby girl."

Even with all the bearish arguing coming from the office, Bygul could hear Cleocatra's purring in response.

Perhaps this romance wasn't doomed after all.

HAVING FINALLY ADMITTED OUT LOUD THAT Jefferson could be her mate, Kate was thrilled when he told her his panther agreed.

Over the next several weeks, they spent all their free time together.

Now that they knew they were mates, they slowed the pace of their romance, getting to know each other and limiting their physical encounters to kisses and heavy petting.

They spent every evening together, sometimes double dating with Nick and Ryan, who had discovered to their mutual surprise, though no one else's, that they were mates.

They also had dinner at the Worcester family home, something Mason insisted happen every Wednesday and Sunday like clockwork.

The first dinner was awkward, to say the least, but after enduring dire threats from Kate, both men had been on their best behavior and so the night had ended with no bloodshed.

Each subsequent dinner was easier and though Kate doubted either man would ever admit it, she thought they were probably growing on each other.

Maybe in another ten years, they'd actually be friends.

When Maggie found out they were having dinner with Mason twice a week, she became extremely insulted on Jackson's behalf and insisted they join her and Jackson two other nights of the week.

Jackson was clearly stunned at this turn of events, as was Jefferson, who explained that Maggie wasn't one for entertaining or enduring people very long.

This, Kate witnessed firsthand, when Maggie just up and left the table mid-way through dinner one night and never returned.

At this point, Kate decided perhaps four nights out of every seven having dinner with family was a bit absurd, so she suggested they invite everyone to Jefferson's house for dinner together instead. By doing it this way, they could cut those days in half and Maggie and Jackson could leave whenever they wanted and not have guests still in their house when Maggie was done socializing.

Jefferson was appalled at the suggestion. "But that means we have to cook!"

Kate rolled her eyes. "Fine. How about this? I make Mason host one night a week and we host the other."

He sighed. "Fine."

So that's what they ended up doing. Every Wednesday, Mason, Jackson, Maggie *and* Genghis Khat came to dinner at Jefferson's place and every Sunday, they all went to Mason's for dinner, *including* Cleocatra.

Everyone else thought bringing the cats into bear territory was a terrible idea, but Kate insisted. She felt it was the least Mason deserved.

The look on Mason's face was quite hilarious when they first arrived, but even funnier was what happened at The Worcester Group the following Monday.

Someone posted in every break room a large photograph of six-foot-eight Mason cuddling Cleocatra.

Kate had no idea how that picture had managed to make the rounds so quickly. She'd texted it to Nick and the next thing she knew, Mason was calling to roar at her for ruining his reputation as a ruthless bear.

Of course, that didn't stop Kate from bringing the cats back the following Sunday.

In fact, she was now contemplating giving Mason a kitten for Christmas, especially since he clearly adored Cleocatra, scooping her from Jefferson's arms the minute they arrived at his place on Sundays and making a beeline for her at Jefferson's place on Wednesday nights.

The most annoying part was that Cleocatra clearly loved Mason as much as he loved her, yet was still prone to crankiness around Kate.

Kate tried wooing her with cat treats and toys and endless petting. Of course, Cleocatra didn't allow the last to happen very often as the kitten had very good Kate radar and would swipe at Kate whenever she got too close.

Still, Kate kept trying and every once in a while, she managed to pet Cleocatra into a purring ball of joy before she realized what was happening.

Cleocatra always gave a little hiss when she finally realized who was petting her, but the hiss was only halfhearted at best, which Kate counted as progress.

All the while she was attempting to woo Cleocatra, Jefferson was wooing Kate. He took her on dates every evening after work and hiking in the woods every Saturday.

Jefferson was clearly much better at the wooing than Kate was, for he took her to every quirky food establishment he could find in the three-city area, making their dates not only fun, but exceptionally delicious.

Kate most heartily approved.

By the time they'd been dating a month, Kate had fallen so deeply in love with her mate, she knew they were meant to be.

This was one mating that would endure for all time.

Which meant, it was past time to let her bear out.

She decided the waterfall where they always ate lunch on their hikes would be the perfect location for their animals to meet.

So, the following Saturday, when they arrived at the waterfall, she stripped naked, stunning Jefferson silent, and dove into the water.

She came up in her grizzly form.

Jefferson let out a whoop of joy, stripped and dove into the water, shifting into his panther form on the fly.

The minute he hit the water, Kate's bear bellowed in triumphant recognition of their mate.

They spent hours in the water, splashing each other and playing, then more hours racing through the woods, chasing each other, each of them taking turns as predator and prey.

Eventually, Jefferson took to the trees and disappeared on her.

She tried to hunt him down, but he clearly backtracked and the next thing she knew, she had a panther on her back.

Even though her grizzly was quite a bit larger than his panther, he clearly didn't mind wrestling her in their shifted forms.

They rolled across the ground, panther and bear, until she eventually allowed him to pin her, then while pinned, shifted back.

She stared up into his panther eyes and watched as they shrank away until he too was in his human form.

She quickly rolled them so she was on top, then kissed him long and deep.

He surged to his feet, lifting her with him.

She wrapped her legs around his waist and held on as he walked them a few feet until her back was up against a tree and then they were kissing again.

Long, endless moments of heat and passion drove them until when they broke apart, they were both gasping for breath.

Staring at each other, he said, "Bed?"

"If we can make it," she said.

Laughing, holding hands, they ran through the woods.

Every once in a while, one of them dragged the other to a stop so they could kiss, caress and fondle before breaking away to run some more.

They reached his house and ran stark naked across the front lawn.

"I sure hope none of your neighbors are looking outside at the moment," Kate gasped, laughing as they stumbled in the front door.

He slammed the door closed, whirled her around and pushed her up against the door, kissing her senseless the entire time.

She surged forward, pushing him up against the opposite wall, still desperately kissing him.

He whirled them past the living room, stopping to press her against the wall opposite the kitchen, then she maneuvered him into the hall where she pressed him against the linen closet and slid a hand down to grope and fondle what she craved so badly.

And so they continued, ever so slowly making their way down the hall, kissing and fondling until they fell into his bedroom and landed on the floor.

They rolled across the floor, nipping and stroking, devouring each other.

She settled on top of him, lifted up and slowly sank down on his cock, taking him one glorious inch at a time.

He groaned and holding her hips, surged upward, thrusting deep.

She cried out in ecstasy and began to ride him.

That first time, they never did make it to the bed, but Kate had no complaints, especially since they did eventually make it there, where they spent the night indulging their passion.

After hours of endless lovemaking, Kate was lying, arm wrapped around Jefferson's torso, head pillowed on his shoulder, cherishing his softly murmured, "Sweet dreams, my love," when Cleocatra landed on her ass, claws fully extended.

Kate let out a grunt, then murmured into Jefferson's chest, "I love you, Jefferson mine. You too, demon kitty."

CLEOCATRA MADE SURE SHE DUG HER CLAWS IN A couple times, kneading the trespasser's skin thoroughly.

She'd never admit it, but she was pretty impressed the bear only grunted a little and didn't try to escape her claws.

When she was sure she'd gotten her point across, Cleocatra hopped from the interloper's butt to Jefferson's stomach, where she padded around, claws retracted—she would never deliberately hurt her Jefferson—until she found the perfect spot on his chest to settle down.

As soon as she was settled, one of his hands came up to stroke her back and scratch her head and chin.

She'd trained him well and now he truly was the best human companion ever.

She was sure, with time, she'd manage to train the bear too.

Of course, the bear was quite stupid so it would probably take her a lot longer to learn exactly how to serve Cleocatra, but no worries.

Jefferson would be around to show her how it was done and Cleocatra was a very good trainer indeed.

Cleocatra fell asleep, purring as she imagined the glory of having two human companions serving her well.

Keep reading for an excerpt from Mason's story,
up next in UNBEARABLY CUTE!

Excerpt

"You want to what?" Jefferson exclaimed incredulously.

"Well, you don't have to say it like that." Kate had no idea why her mate was so astonished. It was a perfectly brilliant idea.

"You're mad," Jefferson said, "and I won't be a party to it. It's cruel."

"It's a kitten, not a torture device."

"Exactly. A poor, defenseless kitten you're planning to feed to your psycho brother."

Rude! Kate let a minuscule roar escape and smirked when Jefferson leapt backwards, clearing the span of the office in one leap.

At the same time, her assistant, Nick, jumped, sending his chair flying out from under him and dumping him on the floor. He glared over his shoulder at Kate, but she didn't know why he was so upset.

It's not like he wasn't used to it by now.

If he didn't like it, he shouldn't sit down in the first place. He had a standing desk for a reason, after all.

Besides, that roar had been halfhearted at best. Why, the windows had barely rattled—she glanced through them to the garage below—and the mechanics hadn't even hit the deck this time.

"I tried to stop her, Cleocatra," Jefferson said mournfully.

Kate whirled and glared at him.

He was cradling his black kitten in his arms, stroking her fur and crooning to her in that way he had, the one that made Cleocatra believe she was the center of his world, something that also made her a holy terror when she felt someone else (usually Kate) was attempting to usurp her role as queen of his universe.

Which, to be honest, Kate did quite often, especially since the way he stroked Cleocatra made Kate imagine all sorts of naughty things involving him stroking her.

"I can't be held responsible for the tragedy to come, Cleocatra," Jefferson said as he slowly stroked his hand down the kitten's back. "I've done my best and now we must all suffer for my failures."

Oh, for heaven's sake. She was surrounded by drama queens. "What are you going on about now?"

Jefferson ignored the question and continued his one-sided conversation with the kitten. "Just remember when the poor kitten gets eaten, or worse, tossed through a window—" he sent a scorching look her way "—it's all Kate's fault."

"My brother would *never*—"

"As someone he's thrown through a window—not once, but twice, mind you—I have to respectfully disagree. *He would.* "

"You were a stranger he'd never met before and you were kissing *me,* his baby sister. What did you expect?"

"Uh, for him to kindly wait until I stopped kissing you and then to introduce himself politely?"

Kate stared at him incredulously. "You do know my brother is an alpha bear, right?"

"So?"

Kate rolled her eyes.

"And while we're on the subject, what about the second time? So maybe he didn't know who I was the first time he launched me through the air, but that second time was pure maliciousness."

Kate turned away so her mate wouldn't see the smirk on her face. "Oh, stop being such a baby. The point is, yes, my brother might toss you around a bit every once in a while—"

"A *bit?*"

"—but he would never hurt a sweet kitten. He adores Cleocatra, you know that."

"I know he's trying to steal her from me," Jefferson growled, "but for what reason I have no idea. What would a psycho–bear want with a tiny kitten anyway? Nothing good, that's for sure."

"Oh, for heaven's sake. Melodramatic much?"

"All I'm saying is maybe you should consider a python or an alligator or — what am I saying? Your psycho brother's the top of every food chain, so really it's better if you choose an entirely different gift for him. No pets for the apex predator!"

Kate snickered. "It's not like I'm suggesting we give him Cleocatra."

The kitten, who was now perched on Jefferson's shoulder, turned her entire body so that she was facing Kate and bared her fangs.

Little monster!

Every time Kate thought she'd finally won the kitten over, Cleocatra went out of her way to prove that she only tolerated Kate and could, in fact, shred her to ribbons at any moment.

Kate lifted her lip, planning to unleash just one of her fangs when she caught sight of the amused look on Jefferson's face and scowled instead.

He should be defending his mate's honor instead of finding amusement in the antics of a tiny little beast who was constantly riling up her bear.

"Anyway," Kate growled, glaring at the two of them, "I'm going to the rescue organization and I'm choosing a kitten for my brother. Are you coming along or not?"

"Not," Jefferson said decisively, as he turned and strode

toward the office door. "Even if I didn't have a garage full of repairs, I still would have nothing to do with this plan to feed a defenseless kitten to that psychotic bear."

"My brother isn't—"

The door slammed, cutting off her protest.

"Dude," Nick said. "You're brother's *so* psychotic."

Kate snickered. "Stop it. He is not."

"Okay, fine. He's out of control, overbearing, outrageously rude... come on, help me out here."

"I mean, all of that is true, but that doesn't make him psychotic."

"No, but throwing people off a cliff kind of does."

"He only ever did that once and it was totally justifiable. Assuming it even happened. I maintain the possibility of his innocence."

Nick raised an eyebrow.

"Besides, Dorian forgave him."

"Eventually. After he woke from that coma. How long did it take him again? A year?"

"Oh, don't exaggerate. It was only ten months."

"What were they fighting about again? Raisinets? Junior Mints?"

"Milk Duds. The last box. I mean, who could blame him? He was a hungry bear. Everyone knows you don't get between a bear and his food."

"But the food was *Dorian's*. And let's not forget that Dorian's a bear too."

"Sure, but Dorian wasn't the *alpha* bear."

"Neither was Mason. At least, not then."

"Are you insinuating that it wasn't obvious my brother was an alpha bear from the moment he let out his first roar?"

Nick made a face. "Okay, fine. Doesn't make it any less psychotic."

"He was five!"

Nick snickered. "And Dorian, how old was he again?"

"Sixteen!"

"Yeah. You do realize none of this is proving him any less psychotic. What kind of five-year old attacks a sixteen year old and wins?"

Kate let out a huff of exasperation. "Isn't it obvious? An alpha bear, of course."

Join Bygul and the other matchmaking cats of the
goddesses as they attempt to matematch this alpha bear,
just in time for the holidays, in UNBEARABLY CUTE.

Other Books by Pepper

THE MURRYSVILLE COALITION

The Crazy Cheetah Lady

One Sad Kitty

A PAWSITIVELY PURRFECT MATCH

Catnapped

The Real McCat

Unbearably Cute

A Catmas to Remember

This Cat's for You

Santa Kitty

Hocus Purrcus

Tridents & Tails

Abra-Cat-Abra

Satan's Kitty

Valen-Cats

Vampurr Lovin'

A Beautiful Cat-ship

Grave Cattitude

THE SHENANIGANS SERIES

Shifter Shenanigans

Witchy Shenanigans

Full Moon Shenanigans

Hotel Shenanigans

Dragon Shenanigans

Undercover Shenanigans

Spooky Shenanigans

Holiday Shenanigans

Valentine Shenanigans

Lucky Shenanigans

STORIES OF THE VEIL

Guardians of the Veil

Astra

Glory

Luna

Zara

WICKED

No Rest for the Wicked

Wicked Is As Wicked Does

Anthologies & Collections

PAWSITIVELY PURRFECT TRILOGIES

THE CAT'S MEOW

Catnapped | The Real McCat | Unbearably Cute

HOLLY JOLLY PAWLIDAY

A Catmas to Remember | This Cat's for You | Santa Kitty

SHENANIGANS ANTHOLOGIES

CRAZED

Books 1-3

AMAZED

Books 4-6

HOLIDAZED

Books 7-10

SHENANIGANS

The Complete Collection

STORIES OF THE VEIL

THE UNVEILED

Astra | Glory

THE VEILED

Luna | Zara

WICKED DUET

WICKED

No Rest for the Wicked | Wicked Is As Wicked Does

About the Author

WWW.PEPPERMCGRAW.COM

PEPPER MCGRAW is a USA Today Bestselling Author of paranormal romance. Her life to date has sadly been paranormal-free, but she knows it's simply a matter of time before her fated mate finally appears. Until that glorious day arrives, she keeps herself busy writing (and reading) paranormal romances.

Pepper loves animals, especially cats, and spends her free time volunteering at local shelters and for Trap-Neuter-Release programs. She's had the supreme honor of winning occasional head butts and meows from the local ferals in her neighborhood and has even convinced a few to come inside and adopt her as their own.

BB bookbub.com/authors/pepper-mcgraw

f facebook.com/ShenanigansSeries

g goodreads.com/peppermcgraw

instagram.com/peppermcgraw_author

tiktok.com/@peppermcgraw

twitter.com/peppermcgraw